Radicalisation

a novel

by

Elizabeth Sinclair

Previously Published
by
Elizabeth Sinclair

Novel
The Evolution of Sarah – 2014

Short Stories

Companions – 2016

The Trip – 2017

The Year of the Diamante Poodle – 2018

Anstock the King – 2020

Front cover: photo by KaLisa Veer on *Unsplash*

ISBN: 9798817276039

First Published (2022)

Vancouver, British Columbia, Canada

"The Wind that Shakes the Barley" - a poem by

Robert Dwyer-Joyce (1836-1883)

Prologue

Fourteen killed. Seven shot in the back. Seven aged seventeen or younger. One belonged to us.

For about the dozenth time I read the executive summary. As a member of the, so called, serious press, I'd received a copy of the 2010 Saville Enquiry as soon as it was released by the British government. The event had been examined for a second time, one of a number of disparate historic tragedies that have been given the name Bloody—honoured with some day of the week—in this case Sunday. For the general population a question of politics or justice, for me, primarily a family matter.

My face had become set in a frown, giving me the beginning of a headache. I moved my glasses onto the top of my head and massaged around my eye sockets and brow. I tipped the most recently filled coffee cup to my lips and turned up my nose.

The findings of the Saville Inquiry contradicted the one that went before. It forced the British Prime Minister to acknowledge the British Army had fired the first shot that resulted in the killing of unarmed civilians on that day. Fourteen killed, none of whom would be found to have the slightest trace of explosives or arms on them.

The interview with his brother, the story of James, stays with me, maybe because it seems so much more murderous than strategic. He told of how his brother had been shot while he posed no threat, then deliberately shot again as he lay on the ground dying. And with him are the many stories of innocents, like our own boy shot in the back while running to find cover. Among the jubilant family members telling their stories in the days following, were the politicians stumbling around in interviews underlining the crucial importance of the Report, their party's regret that it had taken so long to find vindication for the families, making calls for reconciliation.

I want to say, in a knee-jerk fashion, we had been 'caught up' in the tragedy but I immediately stop myself. 'Caught up' implies a lack of will, but active choices were made. Perhaps another person would not have made the life choices Siobhan had possibly made. Maybe a young student, not my mother, would have steered well clear of Northern Ireland in the seventies. Perhaps a young paratrooper at the end of a six-month deployment in Derry would have blinked, or relaxed his trigger finger.

I phoned Mum and Dad a few days after the Report was published. They'd read my article, the one that dealt with the facts, only the facts. Before calling I'd let things settle, find their own level. There were many silences on the call, space for tears I didn't hear falling, but also for sheltering an unstated wish we could shove the whole business back under the bed and never look at it again.

But I can't. For me, the full story does not begin, nor does it end with the events of that day in 1972. Not even by virtue of the latest enquiry. The shockwave that emanates may have begun with a single bullet, but whether we like it or not, rippling from it is another sadness, one I sense rather than see.

I know everything it seems possible to know about that day, at least at a factual level. I'm a journalist, my whole career has been in pursuit of a story, digging around in the facts for what lay beneath. I've never wanted to be just a newscaster. My appetite to go behind the facts of this story may have been whetted long ago by a university project when I first questioned my parents about our family history. Since then, I have felt in my gut we had a hidden story, but I haven't been able to get at it, and I'm constantly confounded by my own family members. I can't empathise with their need to husband their feelings in the dark, quietly, even from each other. The result is, I've not even been able to assess the degree to which the deaths had an impact on them at a personal level. They long ago put up a shield, and I still had to fathom which part of the story they were defending and why. Had I missed something in the telling of Aidan's story? What was it about Siobhan, my mum's friend and my dad's cousin? Was there something else I hadn't picked up to this point.

I only know I seem to be the one who gets most irate about Bloody Sunday. I feel like one of those people who get more enraged by the perpetrators of abuse than do the abused themselves. Why? Couldn't tell you.

My lack of ability to pin my personal fury with precision on the person or persons I feel have done wrong is annoying the heck out of me—not just for Bloody Sunday, but for my parent's reticence to unearth the other layers of the story. I am affronted by it. I cannot help but believe the whole truth lies simmering below the surface and that they know the way into the labyrinth. And I'm maddened by their lack of willingness. I feel the distance this has created.

For some, the Report brought closure but not for me.

As I write, I'm managing to persuade myself that perhaps if I go down the road of re-stitching the story, I'll be able to understand where I've failed before. And perhaps find a way to empathise with their position. I stare ahead, suddenly taken by the fact it will certainly take more courage to directly confront my mother than I've shown to this point. And I know I risk creating distance between myself and my father, whom I adore and admire, but who is like a pit bull when it comes to protecting his beloved wife.

"Good luck," a little voice sitting on my shoulder was saying.

The compulsion to write down my family story isn't recent, but it has morphed since I started to look at the history of Northern Ireland and at how that piece of history worked its way through those closest to me. I've a place in my brain where sits a conviction that examining and writing through the grit of our family lens would be an important addition to the discourse—a perspective on what has become generically known as the Troubles. I have awarded myself a rationale for my drive to pursue this, but lurking in the recesses of my mind is a snake, maybe just a worm, that wants to confront my mother about the very fact of her evasiveness because it goes to the character of a person I love, and whether I have to rewrite what I've always believed about her. It stands against the meals on the table, the boundless support of my failed attempts at sports and her never flinching as I painfully practised the trombone in the kitchen. It does not match with the story she has woven of Dad, of her and me as the people who can rely on each other without question. And those images from my childhood are not squaring with the woman who blows me off when I ask about how Siobhan died. One secret revealing a house of cards we all seem afraid I will blow down.

How can it be so? How is she able to be disinterested about a friend who died in such circumstances?

On calm reflection, I also have to admit there is a fair bit of hubris involved, a belief I can make a better fist of representing an aspect of the story than anyone else. My editor seemed to challenge me on that very point when I spoke to him about my plan.

"Is the question calling out to the journalist or to the self-involved memoirist in you?" he asked.

I could only say, in a way I judge as feeble, "Well, we'll see when I've finished the information-gathering. Right now, I'm not sure the difference matters, not to me anyway."

I was aware as the most recent addition to his department, he'd done me a favour giving me the Report as my brief. In all honesty, it was probably because he knew my background and because he wanted someone with the inside track on the Troubles, not necessarily because he absolutely trusted my skills. I didn't object. After all, I was fresh from submitting freelance articles to local and national papers and working on a blog on political affairs.

For now, I've put the Report away in a desk drawer to start the job of mapping the story in a chronological fashion—in a way that might help me carefully observe and make sense of how things unfolded—the relationships, the why's, the if's, and the potential deceits. And one loud *who*. Who did it to Siobhan?

5

For the moment, I'm in Edinburgh, wearing sweats that should be in the laundry pile, fiddling with the family's chipped, tartan shortbread tin, a picture of the Castle on top in front of me.

The tin is full of old letters, newspaper cuttings, photos, postcards; and in a box file, interview notes I've kept down the ages, with a cassette tape and transcript tucked inside. The latter, the raw data of a project for my degree. These bits and pieces sit with a patchwork memory of overheard conversations, mostly from childhood—those half-told stories drifting around at family events.

Right now, I have an image of my mum sitting at the kitchen table, twirling a tea towel in her hands, and staring into the distance. I'm not sure when it was. She was miles away in thought, brow creased, not hearing when I came into the room. Something made that split-second picture stay with me, feeding the unease in my gut.

Right now, I have that nascent headache, the new software I'd bought on Leith Walk that should make a huge difference to the job of converting spoken word into text and the blinking cursor on the screen, saying 'So, if not now, when?'

1. Robert

Source: From memory
Time Reference: 1946

I'm determined not to gloss over the beginning of the story because I'm in a hurry to get to the tragedy lying somewhere in the middle. These early details, I believe, support the roots of the story and help carry its weight.

And I know Private Robert Buchanan, as well as you can know anyone from merely listening to the stories about a man you've never met. My grandmother had recited the tale in my hearing, when I had disappeared from adult view, probably in a corner of the kitchen reading—the account she gave was of Robert climbing down from a cattle truck about half a mile from the centre of Dumfries and coming to meet her for the first time.

I close my eyes to reimagine the kind of day it was when Robert bowled up—the time and place in history. Raining, I'm sure. I know my hometown well.

As a young man of nineteen, Robert had driven a tank through Austria in the dying days of the Second World War. He would have been used to rides that bumped and hurled their way along. Travelling all night through northern England and into the Scottish Borders would have been easy, his uniform practically guaranteeing him passage, hitchhiking and accepting food and cigarettes from the drivers as he went. The lorry-men were generally too old to have served or had been excused because of the need to maintain food production. They would have welcomed him warmly, shook his hand. All glad to help a young serviceman on his way home from the war.

Robert had disembarked from a ship on the east coast and had made his way through England's industrial centres. Grimy places that stirred memories of his home territory. But for now, he was deep in farming country: grass lanky enough to be cropped for hay; cattle and sheep with heads hanging in the damp early light, nostrils sending steam to join the haar; mile after mile of drystone dykes; and the distant granite houses with a solitary light on the ground floor to signal across the glen the stove was being lit and the kettle put on. He would have mentally logged the villages and small towns, all of which judging by the little I know of his personality, made him feel he was travelling through God's waiting room. Calvinist kinds of places, where the grim reaper brought relief to those suffering a long death from boredom.

Now, the movie is running in my head.

I picture him, turned up jacket collar, an early morning mist coating him, keeping him on the move, searching for the place Margaret had suggested he book into.

Dumfries is the biggest small town around. It's early when he passes a hotel sign, not the right hotel. The place is locked, and no lights offer the hope of human activity. A cafe he finds a little further on also has no sign of life.

A wind picks up and blows a cigarette packet along the pavement ahead. "Bastard," he says to no one, remembering he'd smoked his last.

He walks on and perhaps a man on a bicycle heads toward him. The man is dressed in a black jacket and flat cap and Robert steps out onto the road. The man brakes using the sole of his boot.

"I'm looking for the Burns Inn on Solway Street." Robert says as the cyclist balances himself.

The man speaks from the corner of his mouth, "Soldier?"

"Aye." Robert is irritated by the man's statement of the obvious.

"The bar won't be open for a couple of hours yet. Y'might not find anyone there unless they're expecting you. Street's about a hundred yards down there on the right and the hotel's about a couple of hundred down on the right again."

As Robert thanks him the man adds, "There's a wee place to get breakfast a'fore it, about halfway along Solway Street. You might be best to wait there."

"Fine, thanks for the tip pal. I'm dying for a smoke. Don't suppose you've got a spare."

"Nah," the man said pushing himself off from the kerb.

9

Robert watches him build to a speed he could have beat if he'd set off at a slow jog. He feels unreasonably superior to the country type he'd begged a cigarette from. He's a town boy, lately landed from France, a man headed for an almost blind date. He knows his accent alone, singles him out from the local farm-boys. He draws back his shoulders and hitches his rucksack onto his back. Breakfast sounds good. He hadn't had a decent sausage fry-up since he left home almost two years ago. He picks up his step and lowers his head into the wind.

As he sips his milky tea in the cafe, he lights a cigarette from the pack he'd bought, at the counter and scrutinises the picture Peggy had sent him with her last letter. Her dark hair is pulled back from a round pleasant face and her smile shows a set of teeth he thought would get a girl into films. The head-and-shoulders shot give him no information about her figure. This he has to imagine, hence the blind part of the date ahead.

In a contemporary photo I've seen of my grandmother, she's wearing a sweater that hugged a neck unadorned with jewellery. I would have to say, every inch a country girl.

I wonder if Robert, the city boy, suspected her dancing skills might be limited. Robert is a foxtrot man who no doubt prays there will be a decent dancehall in the town. He could have hot-footed it straight to Glasgow and got there in time for the pubs opening. He was taking a gamble. This little side adventure might be a complete bust, but war had tilted him toward recklessness.

Breakfast done, he looks over his shoulder, standing in the doorway, ready to leave. "Thanks pal, that was great."

He walks to the back of the Burns Inn where he looks for a way in, crates are stacked up beside the door and he takes in a lung-full of the stale beer fumes.

A woman who looked to be in her fifties comes out of the door and they lock eyes as he says, "Buchanan. Got a room booked."

"You're early." She looks at him without dropping the 'what are you doing getting in the way of my morning routine' face.

She says, "Come away in. I'll be with you in a couple of minutes."

He drops his bag on the bare wood floor at the end of the bar and lights a cigarette with a chrome lighter, probably war plunder. When she returns with a hotel register under her arm, drying her hands on a tea towel, he pays for two nights in advance. He intends to leave on Sunday and get back to something he recognises as civilisation.

She shows him a single room—narrow bed, one pillow, threadbare rug, wardrobe, and over a cracked sink, a fly-blown mirror bearing the smears of careless housekeeping—he's slept in worse, including back home.

He nods a kind of acceptance of the terms of his stay and put his bag at the foot of the bed, and as soon as the landlady leaves, he lays down on the bed. After closing his eyes for what he intends to be a few minutes, falls into a deep sleep.

The sun moves as they day progresses, and he wakes suddenly as a weak light breaks through the crack in the curtains. Not quite sure where he is, but relieved the room looks nothing like the interior of a tank, he sits up and immediately sinks back on the bed, allowing time for his breathing to slow. Checking the watch he'd stolen from an unconscious German officer, he realises it's time to wash his face and walk the few yards up the street to meet Peggy.

I'd learned a good part about this meeting third hand from Dad, under the guise of my writing a school essay about what our grandparents did in the war. He'd heard it from Mum and Peggy, probably both at the same time. I learned to rely more on the general rather than the specifics of the story told. I think all of them had an interest in the impression created on the other and particularly with my schoolboy self. But it's a really good story, and I get the distinct impression that Dad couldn't find the edit button as he retold it to me.

I completely believed the arrangement to meet in Dumfries would have begun with just enough intrigue to get Robert's curiosity up. Peggy worked in a factory making soldiers' uniforms. 'For a laugh,' she and her friends had sewed their names and addresses into a few of the jackets. The notes invited the recipients to become a pen-pal. Robert was one of the lucky ones and he responded when he found her name tagged into a seam.

He made a bit of a song and dance of the man-to-man nature of what he was doing. No doubt, in anticipation of the S.E.X bit to follow. I'm recall him filling in enough detail for me to grasp the central point without painting Peggy in a wanton light.

I resume the movie in my head, closing my eyes from time to time to capture the scene and translate into the correct words as I type.

On the day, Peggy and Robert spot each other easily. She shifts from foot to foot. Both wave shyly. It is the immediate post war months. Peggy would have pieced together an outfit from her own clothes and bits and pieces borrowed from friends: leather handbag, cardigan, a violet-coloured dress with bead trimming. I remember the dress from a photo. She notices his red hair and sun-burned face. His cap is tucked into an epaulette.

Robert opens up with something simple, obvious. "Hello, Margaret?"

She asks him to call her Peggy, "Like all of my friends." And she glances up at his face.

"Should we look about for a while, Peggy?" Robert asks.

"Aye," she says walking at his side, and they stroll for a while, past the ironmongers, haberdashery and out of town past the library. The wind dies down and the sky is a clear blue.

Robert gives her a blow-by-blow account of his journey and arrival in the town. Peggy only manages to get a quick word in every now and then.

She jumps in at one point, "Robert Burns is buried over there." And points to St. Michael's Kirk Yard.

"The guy who wrote *Auld Lang Syne*?" Robert asks.

"Aye. He worked in Dumfries at the end of his days."

"Right oh." Swerving around any possibility of being drawn any further into talk of poetry, he ploughs on.

"D'you go out dancing much?"

"Not really. Dalbeattie, where I live, is about fifteen miles from here. We only have a church dance once in a while. The Town Hall here puts on a Saturday night do. But I don't get to it much. The buses stop early."

"What do you do for fun then?"

"I've got a lot of pals. We meet up in each other's houses. Have a laugh. Listen to music, smoke, that sort of thing."

"Well, what're we going to do right now? Is there place you'd like to get a cup of tea?"

"We can go to the Galloway Hotel. They put on a nice afternoon tea. Would you like to see a picture after? I think there's a John Wayne on."

Later, as they wait for her bus home, they make an arrangement for him to visit her parent's place the next day, the plan is then made to head back into Dumfries for the Saturday dance at the Town Hall.

I'm sure in Peggy's version, she gave my parents as much detail as she wanted or dared to. Enough to give shape to the person who turns out to be Mum's biological father. But Mum never offered any of the details to me and I did not push her. She had a way of looking over the top of my head when we entered territory she was uncomfortable with. Dad was the man who would spill the beans, in service of writing the family chronical, and didn't mind passing on the history to me. But he left me in no doubt I was not to trouble Grandma Peggy with questions.

So, I am left with his sketch of the next morning, the rest filled in by my imagination.

I narrow my eyes to start the movie running, Robert is at the front of the bus, hugging his jacket around him, and looking out of the window as the bus bumps its way beyond the limits of Dumfries. It takes him across the county border into Kircudbrightshire and the town of Dalbeattie. When he gets off, his shoulders drooped, he tells Peggy the journey bored him even though it was just over an hour with stops to unload parcels and pick up passengers. He moans about how his backside aches, and he wonders out loud how many of those black and white cows and dirty-looking sheep could be considered entertainment.

He's not been at all captivated by the many shades of green he could count in a single landscape shot. He's glad when he can plant his feet on paving, with no desire to see the verdant land sweeping through Galloway and down to the coast where the Atlantic is funnelled between the coasts of Ireland and Great Britain. He could not be tempted even by knowing on a clear day from Port Patrick he could squint and see the distant coastline of Ireland. As far he is concerned, he'd already reached the town at the edge of the world.

[Note: Dad embellished some of the details as he told the story. I feel sure that was to show to me the man was a complete townie with no appreciation of the finer points of country life. I got the picture.]

But returning to the action, as told by Dad, Robert has a feed of steak pie and potatoes, and they catch the bus to Dumfries in the early evening. Robert regales her again with his tales of hitching his way across country, this after telling his commanding officer he might sign up for the regular army and getting a pass to visit his mother before making up his mind.

He tells her he is dying to get to Glasgow to see which way the wind is blowing, workwise. He adds he might be tempted to go back into service if things don't look great when he gets there.

Margaret allows herself to daydream, believing she could see the years rolling out, with a red-haired soldier husband, finding a cottage for him to come back to when he was on leave. But eventually she looks into the distance to tune out his blethering about Glasgow.

For the dance, she puts on her violet-coloured dress, with a beaded neckline again. She feels simultaneously both proud and a little self-conscious to be on the arm of a soldier.

They pause in the doorway of the large civic room to survey the scene. A draft cuts around their ankles, and cheap cigarette smoke clouds the air. The floor is worn but polished to a dark brown shine. The seats, made of the same wood, are folded out and distributed informally among tables draped in tipsy round tablecloths to hide the rings and chips of wear. The lighting is brighter than the young dancers want but is judged morally correct by the town elders, all stiff collared and corseted, hanging around the edge of the room. I envisage a few of them selling raffle tickets—the prize a leg of lamb.

Robert is relieved this does not appear to be a dance of the jig and reel variety. There is a three-piece band on the stage playing from the American songbook.

Peggy manages to follow Robert's waltz and foxtrot; but he calls a halt at the quickstep and returns her to their seats. He goes to the counter to buy soft drinks, the only liquid refreshment served. He curses under his breath when he realises he's forgotten to put the little flask filled with whisky into his pocket before leaving the hotel room.

Two soldiers in uniform spot a potential brother-in-arms in the young Robert; but he recognises these are not men who had, like him, danced on the ballroom floors of a great metropolis, and apart from their wartime service, he has nothing in common with them. They are returning to farm work. He is heading back home

16

with the world opening up and the only absolute bar, staying out of the coal mines. He gives them monosyllabic answers and puts a proprietorial arm around his date's shoulders.

"You guys ever been to Austria?" Asks Robert.

"Nah. We were on the coastal defence. Never got out of Scotland."

"Too bad. I'm glad I got to see some real action although I could have done without the food dished up there."

One of the guys puts his chin up. "We saw plenty of action. We lost good pals."

Robert decides not to push this any further. Staying on top is the goal. No fights and good patter.

The conversation dries up and they get the message.

Looking at the watch, at 8:20, Robert asks if Peggy would like to stop at his hotel for a sherry before getting the bus home. She feels very adult as they walk to the main door of the hotel.

The next bit of the story telling made Dad lean in, after checking we were alone in the dining room at home where he was telling the story. He told it as if he'd been a fly on the wall. As near as I can remember this is what he said to me.

Robert guides her into a side-room where ladies could sit away from the male domain of the bar, but she can see the local worthies in the public bar through the serving hatch. This was a first time in a pub for Peggy and to boost her confidence, she accepts a cigarette when he returns minutes later with a pint of beer and a sherry. She squints at the portrait of Robert Burns over his head as smoke wafts around and stings her eyes.

Peggy lets him talk about dancing in Glasgow before joining the army, the misery of mining and how he hopes to find a job

17

driving. She doesn't really like his accent. To her ears, it is rough and lacks the musicality of the local lilt, but she admires the fact he's seen and done a lot in his life and has stories to tell.

The sherry makes her face feel hot, and as she hears Robert droning on about Glen somebody or other, a bandleader he particularly liked, she suddenly starts and asks the time.

Robert looks at his trophy watch. The last bus to Dalbeattie is due to leave. They grab their coats and fly out of the door in time to see it sailing past. Peggy starts crying aloud that her dad will kill her.

Robert asks what she wants to do, but Peggy wails and having no other ideas, he puts an arm around her. His mind is clouded with panic.

"I don't think I've got enough to pay for a taxi all that way."

"Oh God!" She wails, "The next bus won't be 'til tomorrow at 8:00."

"I'll get you on the first bus before I take off. It'll be fine, your dad'll understand," he says trying to sound confident. "You can sleep in my room. I'll take the chair," and adds, "We'll need to sneak you in so the landlady doesn't see."

"Oh God," Margaret howls.

"You'll need to stop saying 'Oh God' and keep quiet," he says, annoyance now taking precedence over any other feeling, and he leads her to the back door of the hotel. Peggy creeps up the stairs, choking back tears, stopping every time a stair creaked. She sits on the bed while Robert goes to buy himself another pint in the bar downstairs.

Dad's telling of the next part of the story was accompanied by much coughing, pinking of his cheeks, and checking around to see if anyone else was coming into the room. Sometimes I wonder why he chose to tell me at all. If I had been him, I'd have skipped over it, maybe it was something about my age and the feeling it was time for us to develop a more mature relationship. Maybe he had some foresight my inbuilt curiosity would need feeding with detail sooner or later. Maybe he was right about that. But I like to think the hitherto family chronicler had passed the baton to me, perhaps blissfully innocent of where it would all end.

I imagine he'd learned the story himself when Peggy had taken a few sherries one Christmas and had never spoken of it since.

In the end he plunged on saying, "I wouldn't put this bit in your essay. This is man-to-man stuff, and I'm trusting you to be discreet. Man-to-man, remember."

He didn't need to tell me not to put it in the essay. I would rather have had a tooth out.

Robert returns ten minutes later. Peggy is in much the same position, coat still on. But amid the ensuing kissing and fumbling, Peggy forgets about her fear of what her father would say in the morning.

As Peggy sleeps under the covers, I imagine Robert smoking a cigarette at the open window and concluding the finale of the date was better than he could possibly have hoped for.

Around dawn, the door bursts open and Peggy is shocked from the bed by a father in a full flood. I guess he must have got to know the name of the hotel the day before. He drags Robert from the bed and with concurrent rage for both, tells his daughter to get dressed as he cues himself up to get physical.

In the version in my head, Robert holds up his hands, in a gesture of surrender and he does his best to blurt out the sad story of mistiming the bus and how it was, all his fault, but his explanations are barely heard as the older man lands a punch to his face before he drags Peggy down the stairs by the arm of her coat. All the while, he hurls abuse back at Robert and fumes his way aboard a lorry he'd borrowed from a friend.

In the last scene I have in my mind involving Robert, he rubs his jaw, and packs his bag, and avoiding the landlady, he heads out onto the street and home.

Dad swung back in the chair and said, "thirty-seven weeks later Peggy gave birth to your mother, Rose."

2. Walter

Source: From memory
Time Reference: 1947-1966

Now I've got the first words down on paper, I want to get to my mum, Rose's childhood before I pack up for the night, and go out to buy myself a lamb curry at a place four doors down.

I look again at a couple of pictures lying on top of my desk, the first, a picture of my Great Grandpa from Dalbeattie, flat cap on his head, shirt sleeves rolled up, holding baby Rose. Then, Rose on a pony with two older boys, my uncles, young Walter and Henry, standing beside her, wearing hand kitted pullovers, shading their eyes from the sun. All were tugging at me to remember exactly how

Grandma Peggy and Rose ended up at a farm. The character and personality of young Rose, my mum, hints back to the kind of family, that acted as a crucible for the next part of the story, and the next and then the next. I love how they started to orbit each other as they found their position in the world. How the stars eventually aligned into the constellation I know today.

I remember the story in a muddled, unregulated fashion. It was, after all, never told to me as a complete narrative. But I recall the questions careening back and forth in rooms smelling of coal fires and lavender furniture polish, sometimes they were looking for clarification and sometimes to remark at Grandma Peggy's boldness as a young woman. I look again at the pretty woman in the photograph album, no adornment, yet with a confidence born of having survived winters and summers of rationing at a time when her country had been at risk of invasion.

I have figured out that baby Rose stayed in the care of her grandmother, my great grandmother, while Peggy worked in the local butcher's shop. The factory that had employed her during the war years had been decommissioned by the time of Rose's birth and was being allowed to slowly sink into ruin. Even the crater outside of town, carelessly created by a German bomber heading for the shipyards on the River Clyde in 1941, had begun to grass over. Rose was perhaps the only memento Peggy had of those early post war years, and Robert had left no forwarding address.

As Peggy's pregnancy had progressed, her mother grudgingly adapted to the shame she perceived had been visited on her. Step one had been an abrupt withdrawal from church attendance. Steely haired and tight lipped, she quietly returned to regular worship about a year after the birth. The first wave of tittle-tattle had by then dried on the lips of the gossips. I heard how she held her head up, and politely thanked people for their enquiry as she rejoined the members of the upstanding congregation in her previous Sunday pew. I got the picture. She wanted the shame to disappear into the recesses of the Christian community's archive as soon as possible and discouraged if not outright forbade Peggy's attendance at the service.

Great Grandma, I gather, had been an unenthusiastic child minder. Under her care, Rose was kept fed, dry and out of harm's way but she never showed the child affection. My Great Grandma's primary focus became a determination Peggy should work to feed and clothe the child she had inflicted on the family.

By contrast, I am told, Rose had my Great Grandpa in her thrall. Forgotten was the day in Dumfries when he'd landed a solid punch on the face of the soldier-laddie. Rose was his joy, dark haired like his own mother. She had round cheeks which he loved, and they spoke to him of days of plenty, the end of wartime deprivation. Rose toddled toward him when he came home through the back door of the terraced house. She didn't mind his smell of earth, fertiliser, and cow barn. He picked her up, invariably telling her they must wait to have a bit of toffee until after their tea and swinging her around until she broke into giggles.

I imagine him saying, "Peggy, this child needs shoes. I'll leave you money to buy her some on your day off. Get her some of those nice red ones." Great Grandma no doubt drove a look into the side of her husband's head which he chose to ignore.

I was told Peggy bought the local paper on the day she bought the shoes and noticed the advertisement for a live-in housekeeper. The position was on a farm close to Dumfries, on the road leading to Castle Douglas. There was a telephone number and the name Walter Cameron. Peggy chewed on her thoughts for a whole day. Would Farmer Cameron be willing to take a woman with a two-year old child? Would he doubt her suitability? Would she be able to convince him she could keep a house when she had never lived away from home?

Without consulting a soul, she phoned Walter Cameron the next day. She told him her name, her address in Dalbeattie and that her father was a dairyman. This was enough to get her an interview. It took some pleading to get her mother to look after Rose and it required telling the tale she was in pain and needed to see a dentist. If the farmer would not have her, she did not want to have alerted anyone in the family of her escape plan. So, she forgave herself the small invention.

On the day of the interview, the Dumfries bus dropped Rose off where the road from Dalbeattie met the road to Castle Douglas and she walked the remaining mile to the Cameron farm. She was punctual, dressed in sturdy leather shoes and the silky, mauve headscarf her parents had given her for Christmas. It was the only nod to the dreams of glamour she had put behind her. She carefully walked up the rutted drive and decided to knock at the back door set in three-foot thick granite. The front door's for guests, she told herself and she did not classify herself as a guest. She painted a vivid picture in the retelling I'd heard, of a man with a broad chest and hair greying prematurely at the neck and temples who answered her knock. He looked to her to be in his mid-thirties, wearing a thick cotton shirt, green corduroy trousers and work boots. Walter Cameron wiped his hands on a rough towel saying something like,

"You'll be Peggy," gesturing her inside and before she had a chance to answer. "You're a bit younger than I imagined."

They sat at the kitchen table.

"I expect, but I'm hard-working." I see her letting the head-scarf slip off her head.

What remained with Peggy was his steady gaze, taking her in, asking questions.

"You live in Dalbeattie—why the move? House keeping's not what young lassies usually go for."

She'd prepared some answers, wanting to sound confident.

"The truth is, I'm keen to move out of my parent's house and I don't see a way unless I get a live-in position."

"And you've never kept house before?"

"No, but I cook, clean, and do laundry right now. I know I can do it."

Peggy confessed during the retell she was impressed with the place. The farm kitchen was big, the heart of the house, with a coal fired stove. The floor was stone, clean but not scrubbed and dishes were piled in the sink. She could still smell ham, and strong tea from a pot bubbling on the hot plate.

Walter filled her in on the details. "You should realise I've two children. They're four and eight, both boys. They're a handful and I'd want the housekeeper to watch out for them too. My wife died a year back and my parents are both dead. My sister, Lizzie, was seeing to us but she has a young man now and wants to get married."

"I'm sorry to hear about your wife. It must've been hard on your boys." This was the big moment in the story and she remembered she took a quick breath before adding, "I've a girl of two, Rose."

"Aye."

Apparently, he managed to create enough space with that word for a moment or two of thought. And then said," What are you going to do with her if you move in here?"

In my imagination, Peggy would have fiddled with some crumbs on the tabletop. "I was hoping to bring her here with me."

When she looked up, she saw a smile as he shook his head. "Now that's something I'd never even thought about."

Peggy told how she managed to look right at him, she sensed there was no moralising in what he said, none of the kind of judgement she'd feared. She felt she had a chance to make her case.

It is hard not to admire the way she apparently had her answer ready. "I know it sounds like a huge cheek for me to be asking, but you need to know I'm clean. My girl is potty-trained and quiet. Like most women, I'd be doing for the children and keeping the house at the same time. No different than any married woman does. The only difference is you can give me the sack if it doesn't work out and you can pay me less for the cost of keeping my girl."

He ignored her on the money issue. "How do you think you'd manage taking on two boys as well as your daughter? You'd have your work cut out for you."

"I'm young, just twenty-three. I've loads of energy. I've worked since the day I left school. I've got three brothers. I promise I can make the best steak pie you've ever tasted. I'll make sure you never regret taking me on."

Walter stopped, giving himself time to reflect. "I need to think about this, Peggy. Why don't you telephone me tomorrow? Let me sleep on it. It's a big decision."

"That's fair," she says, not feeling optimistic in the moment. She had wanted him to say "yes" there and then, but lifted her chin to avoid showing disappointment. Walter watched as she made her way out to the road. He liked her and said later he always knew she would be a breath of life around the house. His boys needed someone with some energy about them and maybe this young person would be better than the middle-aged farm type he'd had in his head. But, the story goes, he took the time he'd given himself and made his way out for the afternoon milking.

The next morning, after he got the boys off to school, he phoned his sister. He felt the need to talk though the decision with his most trusted adviser.

Her first reaction had apparently been to advise him he'd be taking a bit of a risk, "Will she take care of her own daughter at the expense of your boys? And will she be able to handle a big farmhouse, cooking and tending to the children?" She paused, "There again, would an older lady have the energy? Have you seen anyone else you've taken to?"

"I've seen three others and I didn't warm to a single one of them. She's the first one without the hard-edge I worry about."

He stopped and his sister let him think on the other end of the phone.

"I'm going to give her a month's trial. Should be enough to see how things are working out. She can always go home to her folks if it doesn't."

She didn't say a word and let him go on. "See, I knew I'd sort this out if I talked to you. Thanks Lizzie." He put down the phone, relieved he'd come to a decision.

When Peggy phoned, she agreed to start after she'd worked a week's notice at the butcher's shop. As she hung up, she tells of doing a little jig in the phone box. She liked the idea of living on the sprawling farm, in the comfortable granite house and for baby Rose to live and grow up in the company of other children.

Now she needed to tell her parents. That, no doubt, put a temporary damper on her delight.

The remonstrations went something like, "It's not respecta-ble Peggy, living with a man you're not related to. It's a job for an older woman with more sense in their head and not likely to attract wagging tongues."

"Sorry Ma, my mind's made up. I need to let you have your lives back and I want a fresh start. Dumfries isn't far away. I'll bring Rose home for visits and you won't miss the noise and the mess, I'm sure."

Rose's Dad shook at the newspaper he was reading. "You'll both be missed," he said into his chest.

Her mother sniffed and said, "Some hope of a fresh start wi' a bairn in tow."

This point in the story is a good place to stop and attend to my hunger pangs. I find my shoes beside the door, and I walk, doing what I normally do, talking to myself, churning over the details I had worked on or would tackle tomorrow.

The next day, barefoot and dressed in the same sweats, I sit down in front of the laptop. It's a new day and I'm ready to pick up the threads of the story. I plug in the laptop to keep it charged, and I get down to writing.

After a slow courtship conducted under the same roof and accompanied by much tongue-wagging in the community Peggy and Walter, my grandparents married quietly. The Minister looked down his nose but comforted his Calvinistic soul with the conviction he was bringing the sinners back into the fold of the godly.

I believe Walter took charge of the burgeoning relationship by insisting Peggy accompany the family to see films in the local cinema and buying her chocolates to enjoy. He seemed to think the way to her heart was through her stomach because he bought her chocolates for her next birthday. He got her flowers from all three of the kids living with them for Mother's Day. The big move, I understand, was made by taking her to dinner and a summer evening ride on a friend's boat on the Solway. I did learn she made the bold move to take his hand when they walked back to the car park from the shore that evening. Anything else would be guess work and although I lack detail, it's clear over time, there was a very short engagement and the family continued to blend through rubbing along day-to-day. I know my grandmother. She would have won them over with kindness and an impish sense of fun.

As far as I know, Rose only ever regarded Walter's sons as full brothers: young Walter—truly his farming father's son, Henry—the studious one. The 'step...' prefix never crossed her lips. In turn, they called Peggy, Mum, and I was told the only time Walter ever raised his voice in a true rage was when one of them, I wouldn't know which, stormed out of a scolding telling a tearful Peggy he wished she had never moved in and she was only the housekeeper.

29

Whatever happened over that first-year or so, the result was a seamless loving group, and by the time of the next big event, probably told only once in my presence, the picture is clear. Again, I can run the events of that day like a movie playing in the middle distance. I know the house well, the field, the view over the Galloway Hills. I've spent many days of my own childhood days there.

It's no problem for me to place the actors on the stage: my mother Rose, young and carefree riding her sturdy black and white pony with the black mane in the grass paddock across the lane from the house. She's wearing a faded, black velvet riding helmet, her cheeks are flushed as she puts Jacko, through his paces, pretending to hear the applause of the crowd at an imaginary gymkhana as she rides to take the first-place ribbon.

Suddenly, she feels weak, not just hot from the exertion of the ride or from the morning sun. She dismounts, lets go of Jacko's reins and manages to make it to the gate before collapsing. When she eventually rallies, soaked in sweat, Walter is carrying her through the back door into the kitchen where he sets her down on the worn sofa under the window.

"What happened?" Peggy shouts.

"I don't know. I found her on the ground."

"Did she fall?"

"I don't know, my love. Now, you watch her, and I'll call for the doctor to come out."

Peggy feels Rose's forehead. She is burning up. My grandmother soaks a cloth in cool water from the tap and mops her brow.

"What happened?" She asks Rose when she opens her eyes.

"I don't know. I felt hot, and when I got off Jacko, I had a bad pain in my tummy. Then I don't remember what. Is Jacko okay?"

After what must have seemed like an unbearable wait, Walter answers the door and leads the doctor through to the sitting room where Rose has been moved to wait for his arrival. Henry and Young Walter sit drained of colour, eyes wide staring at their sister who now lies tossing her head from side to side, occasionally muttering words they can't catch.

After an examination the doctor looks grave. The soft lowing of the cows outside—an indicator afternoon milking is near—is the only sound as everyone holds their breath, waiting on his words.

"We'll need to do more tests but I'm very concerned. Let's get her to the hospital and work at keeping her fever down. We'll know more after that."

Rose had missed the polio-vaccine appointment when Peggy took the boys. Instead, she had ridden Jacko to a pony-club competition that summer's day. The postponed immunisation had been scheduled for the week after she fell ill. In payment for the bad timing, Rose spends twelve weeks in the infirmary's stark, tiled, colour-resistant polio ward. Peggy and Walter are barely allowed to visit and receive only brief updates from a starched ward sister. No one in the family truly rests.

The women in the church choir deliver pies to the farm door, everyone prays for a full recovery.

I was reminded as I looked at the photos that life went on. Things happened. Life happened that I did not personally witness but heard of through my mother. The family went through the trauma of having a sick child at home and all the usual fun and pain of growing up.

Young Walter and Henry, both dark haired, tanned, and muscular in those photographs went back to school before Rose was discharged from hospital. After two more months she was allowed to continue her convalescence at home. Rose's grandpa caught the bus into Dumfries every weekend and stayed at the farm, visiting his 'wee treasure' as often as he felt he could.

It was decided she should take the rest of the school year off and start afresh in the class of younger kids the following September. Peggy was not unhappy about this. Both the time off to recuperate, and the prolonged protection from the boisterous activities of the kids were blessings as far as she was concerned.

During her time in the infirmary, Rose had physically shrunk before the eyes of the entire family. No one took pictures, but Peggy painted the picture for us in her retellings. When she came home, Rose limped in calipers which encased legs so thin it caused Peggy pain to look at them. She used child-sized crutches and people stared when she went with her mother to shop in the town. Walter massaged her legs each night before bed, willing strength from his warm calloused hands into her limbs. Grandpa suggested broth, milk, honey, and anything else he could imagine would put some meat on her bones. Peggy fed her hearty stews and buttered potatoes.

The retelling of this part of the family story is replete with detail of how they slowly allowed for hope when Rose could walk along the farm's rutted tracks using two walking sticks. She stumbled and tensed but all the while she gained back essential mass in her withered muscles. By the Spring she was able to ride Jacko at first led by one of her brothers.

The whole household fussed and coddled, sometimes to the point of enraging her. The boys attempted to ease the burden of her boredom by telling her she was lucky not to be at school, and subject to the rigours of fractions and the poetry reading they had to endure. Henry loaned her his *Boys Own* comics, worrying she would forget how to read. Peggy and Walter hovered and quietly gave thanks she had survived and had come through the illness in a way many were unable to.

I lean back in my seat, pausing to stare at a black and white picture in the album in front of me. Beneath it says, 'Taken to celebrate the day Rose walked into church without the aid of crutches or sticks for the first time,'

Rose is dressed in a flowery print dress and a cardigan, no doubt knitted by her mother. She has ordinary-looking shoes that look white, the same colour as her ankle socks. There is still the tell-tale presence of calipers and she's holding Walter's hand. The ladies of the church choir are looking on from the back.

I flip to a school photo. I can see Rose was frail and smaller than her twelve schoolmates when she started back at the country school. But, in the one-roomed building, any hierarchy involving the year she was in was almost certainly deemed irrelevant. She was part of an undifferentiated pool of learning supervised by an enthusiastic young woman who had recently married the owner of the local forge.

No doubt, everyone was curious about where she had been all year and about the hardware attached to her legs, but I imagine that was about the extent of it, and in time, she told me, she

33

learned to enjoy being the oldest and most interesting in the group of students.

And as she grew in height and strength, the calipers were left behind. Polio left only one scar that lasted through her life, the slight limp I know well, and which becomes pronounced when she is tired.

When Rose graduated and started high school, Peggy and Walter had been man and wife for eight years. Rose was clever, could take part in most school sports and was riding a larger pony called Prince who became the elder statesman of the paddock I knew from my own visits to the farm. I remember his brown coat and the dark fringe hanging down rakishly over one eye.

A fourth child had been added to the family, a boy called Thomas who was aged five in the year she left him behind at the primary school. Young Walter was by then going to agricultural college and Henry was three years ahead of her in high school.

From family lore, I can tell Rose, Mum, was the girl who stood at the centre of her group of brothers. She tenaciously tended and reinforced the bonds among them. She was the one who knew what was going on in all of their lives. She prompted them about birthdays. She chivvied them about keeping their parents informed and reassured about their lives, even if Walter and Peggy didn't make a fuss or bombard them with questions.

I can't help thinking of Rose as a fairy story character: struck by polio, beloved of her family, bossy, charming, and totally uncomplicated. The photo album is testimony to my impression. Rose, usually at the centre, grabbing a brother in an awkward hug. I remember one shaky home movie where she is handing out the Christmas gifts from under the tree.

I loved to drag the family stories out of my mother. I learned it was Henry who watched her closely during her school years and who would be the one to bloody the nose of her first boyfriend. Thomas was her pony-riding buddy and had inherited the faithful Jacko. As she grew, both the young and old Walters allowed themselves to be bossed by her. She made sure they changed to look presentable when the clothes they wore around the farm were not going to pass muster. Peggy deferred to her taste in these matters, no doubt wondering if the genes of her dapper biological father were seeping through.

My mother remembers those times, the 1959 bi-centenary of the poet Robert Burns which coincided with the year she started at the eponymous high school. She told me this story when I was about to go to high school, in the same building. The tall cherry-wood cabinet, still there, faced visitors walking through the main door. It housed a darkly-framed portrait of the Bard. The picture captures a youth and vitality which probably never faded because he did not live to old age.

That year the display included a manuscript of 'A Man's a Man for A'That', which the local museum had loaned to the school for the academic year.

In a nod to posterity, she told me, the first-years learned to recite 'To a Mouse'. Mr. Hendry, who taught English, did not miss the opportunity to guide the class in burrowing below the surface image of a cute rodent. He gave them an appreciation of the creature as a metaphor for the status of man. They learned about Burns as an early man of the Scottish Enlightenment and the vehement anti-slaver, not the indolent poet and lover of the ladies. The end-of-year prize-giving ceremony featured Rose's class rendering the

35

poem in full. She was chosen to recite the stanza which lays bare the pain of the mouse at being turned out of house and home. Rose had only ever known the security of a close family living on land it owned. Burns provided her with her first insight to the possibility of a less perfect world, both in the experience of her ancestors, and among people of her own age who were less fortunate. I believe it lay dormant for a few years until circumstances prodded the message awake.

And ever a man to create a lasting impression, Burns accompanied Rose throughout her academic career. He seasoned her high school labours over literature and Scottish history. He seemed to be at her elbow when she chose to study modern history and English literature at St. Andrew's. On the last day before she left to travel to the university, she placed a symbolic red rose in front of the Bard's mausoleum in St. Michael's Church yard—on the stone bearing one word—

Burns

3. Rose and Siobhan

Source: From memory
Time Reference: 1966 – 1970

Straight from thoughts of Burns, I'm propelled to thinking it must have taken an act of providence for Rose, my mum and Siobhan to have found each other in their earliest days at university. In front of me, resting on my keyboard, is a picture taken on the day of their graduation. Goofy poses. Written below, "Henry catches Siobhan and me on Graduation Day."

At the outset, they'd been assigned to the same student residence in St. Andrews and although they didn't share a room, were taking some of the same classes.

Curious about how they made friends, I listened to what Mum had said in the past over many suppers or evenings spent with the grandparents. Mum always speaks in an upbeat way, about those early days, with no hinting at the drama to come. I've never seen my dad contradict or question her. If he has his own view of the women's relationship, he keeps silent. At family meetings, he often sits like a sphynx nursing a beer as others talk. To be fair, he didn't know Mum in the St. Andrews days, and he leaves her to her own characterisation of the relationship the two women had. I've never challenged or second-guessed any of this—until recently. I believe, intuitively, Mum never wanted her memories corrupted by the questioning of a sceptical son. There were never conversations in the past, only ever what could be called information sessions. And, whatever Dad's take might have been on the events has never been probed by me. I'm curious if it has ever been tested between them. I wonder if this is typical of people who've lived through trauma—believing it is better to leave alone anything that might cause trouble if brought into the light.

Honouring Mum's reluctance to be more forthcoming, I've always skated on the surface rather than digging further into the story of her and Siobhan as young women. However, with my suspicion that there is an actual betrayal at some later point in this story, the whole of their past has taken on a different significance, as I wonder if there is something that is connected to how Siobhan died. I now have a new resolve to investigate and dig even if it is uncomfortable.

I look at the photos from St. Andrews again, trying to read into the body language in those small snapshots. They were maddeningly benign.

Siobhan looks wholesome and unfettered by worry. I understand from Mum she was very open about following a personal plan to consciously leave her home in Northern Ireland to get a higher education. For the benefit of her Catholic family, she had emphasised the quiet tradition of the university and kept had quiet about St. Andrew's role in the Protestant Reformation. The picture created for me by Mum was she was relieved to be on the sandy east coast with her back to Ireland and her face turned toward the continent of Europe. I can't help but wonder if her equivocation was an early sign of slipperiness.

Mum told me Siobhan began to eschew Mass the day she landed. It seems she was determined to be just another girl from the provinces—a young woman away from home for the first time, a child of the sixties with less time for organised religion and more of a passion for the humanities. She confided in Rose a desire to grow into womanhood without her mother's fussing and her older brother Brendan's vehement hatred of the British. The young, recently emancipated Siobhan was leaning toward a single degree in history but keeping her options open by joining Rose in the first-year course in modern English literature. Although from different backgrounds, their educational paths and critical thinking were merging. Siobhan talked of how she craved a broader palette of words and thoughts than had been offered by her former immersion in Catholic saints and Irish writers. For her, Shaw, Goldsmith, and St. Thomas Aquinas had been approved and had served to whet her appetite. Oscar Wilde, on the other hand had been demonised. Mum brought with her the rebel, Burns.

In those early days, when Mum was only beginning to make Siobhan's acquaintance, she told me of how she was revisited by the loneliness she'd felt on the polio ward. She worried about not fitting into a crowd, and about her lack of exposure to the swinging decade she had heard other girls talking about. She had shown me a photograph from that first winter. Her appearance probably drew no particular attention. She dressed her slim frame in trousers and sweaters. A navy-blue duffle coat buffered her against the wind of the North Sea. In the photo, her hair was swept back, fastened at the neck, a style which emphasised her frail features and pale complexion.

"Look at me," she had said. "I look like a country girl compared to the others in short dresses, with their asymmetrical haircuts." And you know, for the first two weeks of the term I spoke to Mum or Thomas on the phone every day. I wanted to hear their voices. I used to keep them talking by asking questions about the ponies' diets and whether they were giving them enough exercise. Then for good measure, I'd ask Peggy to check I'd returned all my library books."

I could imagine the conversation in the farmhouse after she rang off.

"I think she's lonely, Walter."

His reply would be soothing. "Try to let her be. She needs to get used to things. I'm sure she'll ask if she needs something."

I ate up the stories of Mum's early student days and I learned the genesis of the relationship that developed between her and Siobhan as they walked to lectures in the windy, granite town. How they eventually joined the student dramatic society and were immediately pitched into *Pygmalion*. I imagine Siobhan thought, "Bernard Shaw again."

Nevertheless, Mum told me Siobhan felt she had the cultural upper hand that should have made her the obvious choice for the part of Eliza Doolittle, but her mainly English cohorts did not agree. They thought a woman called Pamela, she of slim build, blond hair and blue eyes, could do a better job of mastering the dual challenges of pulling off the cockney and cultured accents the part required. Siobhan had complained she was sure her dark hair, lack of height and the light dusting of freckles on her face had not won her points when it came to securing the lead role. At the end of the casting-call, Rose and Siobhan were awarded minor walk-on parts.

"Did she hold a grudge?" I asked.

"Not in the least. We shrugged it off."

I am told in the end they convinced themselves they were lucky at not having to learn any lines, while being legitimately admitted to the parties held in the flats of other cast members.

One of the days when we talked, Mum tugged at my shirt sleeve drawing me in as she lowered her voice, "At the celebration to launch the first night we both got drunk and staggered home to the hall of residence trying not to attract attention as we crept in."

"Rebel," I said and supressed a smile. She had no difficulty with these small confessions, or maybe she used them to deflect from any deep enquiry about other things later. As if saying, I'm totally open. Nothing to hide or feel uncomfortable with. This had always drawn me in, and I went along with the story of unblemished friendship.

I understand my mum well enough to know that regardless of her new life, she maintained the links with her family. There must have been weekend chats when she could reach Peggy, Thomas and sometimes even Henry or Young Walter. I'm sure they got the edited version of her exploits as a student, a new woman of academia. They would have been relieved to hear about her friendship with Siobhan and in the expanding form their love took would have begun to look forward to meeting her.

It was obvious from her course of study subjects, that her attachment to Burns was growing. This had been encouraged by the presence on faculty of Henry Stewart, a Burns scholar with an international reputation. From her first year she told me how she made it her business to learn about his academic career. I suspect the idea of being his favourite would have appealed to her. After all, she was accustomed to being teacher's pet. But this was university, and to pursue her accomplishment as a literary scholar, she knew she must broaden her horizons. Burns was not part of her first classes on modern authors, and it was not until second year that she could legitimately insert her man into an assignment. She had often talked to me about immersing herself in his Enlightenment ideas and appreciating his strong ethical compass. Daringly, I once questioned her about how his moral compass didn't include fidelity when it came to his marriage and the women in his life. She came back at me in a snap.

"He had a clear idea of Rights written with a capital 'R' and a hatred of hypocrisy. Somehow, he could hold the standards guiding his personal behaviour separate from his beliefs in how society should be organised, and do so with no sense of moral conflict. I

42

like to think he had a certain level of responsibility and a coherent set of standards, even if I don't know for sure what they were."

Sitting at the table in the family dining room window alcove that morning in the light of a spring day, she reminisced with me about a project that asked the class to reach back as far as the late 1700s, to find examples of humanist themes in poetry and literature. Siobhan, she told me, chose the County Limerick poet Robert Dwyer-Joyce. She had told Rose about her mother's love for his song, *The Wind that Shakes the Barley*. She painted for me, over a glass of red wine, the scene where they sat in animated discussion on the historical perspectives of the two men born a hundred years apart. They were joined by Pamela, who had played Eliza in Pygmalion. She added William Blake to the conversation.

"Everyone knows the hymn Jerusalem," she had said, "But did you know Blake wrote the words after he saw a child chained by an employer to an iron manhole cover so he couldn't run away? English people can get riled about social justice too."

With their relative strength in Celtic-number, Rose and Siobhan refused to concede the point. Siobhan spoke up.

"You mean the English suffered at the hands of the English too? What a shock! But never mind Pam, spend time with us, and some of our Celtic sensibility's bound to rub off. After all, you've come to a Scottish university, at some level, you must have wanted to shake off the almighty English yoke."

"I came here because neither Oxford or Cambridge would have me," she said, only half-joking, red-faced, and not being absolutely sure if she had said something that reflected badly on herself.

One topic apparently led to another, and I got another insight into the kind of friendship they had formed.

"Well think yourself bloody lucky you got lucky and arrived here," said Siobhan probably only half-joking, and immediately seeing an opening which allowed her to ask a favour.

At this point, she asked if she'd be willing to drive them all in her car because she needed to go on a trip to Lanarkshire to visit a model village for an assignment she was working on. She dangled the promise of seeing the work of another man of the Enlightenment who wanted to ditch the legacy of the "Dark Satanic Mills."

Pamela was obviously curious enough to agree but only if they could eat out at some point. Pamela said she was already sick and tired of the food in the halls of residence.

From this, I began to get a sense of the developing social conscience of the pair. Mum said Siobhan's impetus for making the trip was an essay assignment on the Model Village Movement. New Lanark being close enough for her to visit and photograph. She intended the piece to help her gather the momentum necessary to get a place on the Honours Degree course in modern history. With the need for a solid 'A' for Siobhan, and the thought of a high tea somewhere *en route* for motivation, the three women set off on a fine, dry Sunday in November with a borrowed camera. The adventure would have taken them over the River Forth skirting past Edinburgh, across miles of moorland and bubbling rivers into rural Lanarkshire. Pamela stayed in the car reading while Siobhan and Rose carefully threaded their way among the decaying buildings. They met three teenagers, a girl and two boys who had arrived as they were leaving.

Mum told me of the banter in the car, reliving a treasured time.

"I wonder what their story is," Mum had said as they drove away later, "it's not exactly a prime tourist destination."

"Who knows," Siobhan said, repacking the camera, "Maybe they have a body in the car they need to dump."

"Not likely, they looked too young and innocent. I think it's more likely they're brothers and sisters looking for the grave of their long-lost grandfather who died in a horrific mill accident," Pamela contributed.

Mum warmed to the magical thinking, "Maybe they are the ghosts of three teenagers who drowned while swimming in the River Clyde."

"Don't be daft," answered Siobhan. "Who would be crazy enough to risk freezing to death swimming there in the first place. Maybe they're anarchists looking for a place to store their bomb-making equipment."

Mum paused almost imperceptibly. I remember in hindsight, the hesitation just before she shook her head to clear her thoughts.

"What're you thinking?" I asked.

"Nothing at all," Mum answered.

Mum even remembered the meal in Moffat as being the time when the three came to an agreement they would move out of residences and into a flat in the next year. Mum didn't want to ask her parents for the extra money it would involve, and this was the point when she first took a summer job instead of helping around the farm. The ladies in the church choir were her main net-work and a job was found.

For Siobhan and Rose the time at St. Andrews went by, in my thinking, as a fleeting and yet profound youthful experience. They followed through on the plan to flat-share with Pamela and were able to have boyfriends visit. At some point, I heard about Rose's wine lighted candles stuck into raffia-wrapped wine bottles. Romance seemed fragile and futile, as each transient affair fizzled out after trial, error and disappointment. Their friendship was never truly threatened by local males. During term time, even Pamela forgot about a young man back in London whom her parents thought of as husband-material.

The rest is an undifferentiated blur to me until Mum invited Siobhan home to the family farm for the Christmas holiday in the year before they graduated. To me, this underlined a closeness that had been kindled over the years. I am as sure as I know anything, the young Irish woman would have been embraced by the family and its traditions during the stay. The tree in the front room would have been decorated for their arrival, beds would have been aired and beaten into neatness, and there would have been enough food in the house for twenty people.

I heard a conversation between Rose and Siobhan much later, when I was a young eves-dropper, about how Mum enjoyed having another female presence in the house to balance the male dominance there. They laughed when they talked about the time they shared Mum's teenage bedroom, decorated with posters with the text of Martin Luther King Junior's *I Have a Dream* speech, and the face of Robert Plant.

Although she no longer sang in the church choir, Rose took Siobhan to the Christmas Eve carol service. The songs resounding through the spare Presbyterian timbers would have been loved regardless of their separate religious traditions.

She taught Siobhan to ride during the visit. Jacko was brought out of the barn where he was spending his semi-retirement and I picture him gently bearing the inexperienced friend of the family on his broad back—the women wrapped in woollen coats and scarves, walking the horses along the grass shoulder of the Castle Douglas Road and then meandering on horseback through the paths and trees down to the freezing Cargen Water. I have to acknowledge this scene gets its detail from my own experiences rather than any first-hand telling.

I can't say when exactly, but it is clear, at some stage they passed the point of having a superficial friendship. This was evident even to someone like me, picking up information in dribs and drabs.

Mum took delight in telling me how her handsome and shy brother, Henry, took a shine to Siobhan and volunteered to lead Jacko as she practised. It all seems too light-hearted in the retelling. She said they managed to supress any urges to tease or play practical jokes on him as they chatted between themselves. But his anxious queries about Mum's romantic exploits were consistently rebuffed. Those intimacies were kept for the ears of girlfriends, not of older brothers. Henry was more successful in securing a promise from Siobhan to write to him after the visit.

The ties that were to bind Siobhan and my family were multiplying, deepening. To this day, and in spite of everything else I've learned about her, I find it hard to grasp how at some point in the future, she must have made a conscious decision to set those relationships aside. When the going got tough for her, it seems she chose not to use the support she had formed and nurtured?

The questions rear up early. Why did she betray those closest to her? And I determine that betrayal is deeper than its first cousin, lying. It robs the victim of something profound—quite often a confidence in their own judgement, or in the truth of their memories.

More particular to my family's story, is why is my mother was either oblivious to a betrayal or profoundly forgiving? And why can't we talk about it now I'm a grown man? What is it that threatens to emerge when that blindness is challenged by digging behind the bereavement or fears of treachery?

From the point of that Christmas holiday on, I believe things changed between the women. No more casual girl stuff. Everything that characterised the relationship became more profound, intense, adult.

It was important for me to know if Siobhan ignored her family over the holiday. Was she showing she could easily compartmentalise her life? I phoned Mum who thought it an odd question but confirmed Siobhan had phoned home to Derry on Christmas Day. I pictured in my head her watching my uncle Thomas, going about his youthful business around the house or going off with his dad on one mucky exploit or other, and this prompting the need to make contact with her mother and brothers.

Her own brother, Aidan, was a year younger than Thomas, but photos show they both had a similar awkward teenage look, wearing jeans they couldn't keep from sliding over their hips. I could see how she wouldn't have wanted young Aidan or her mother to feel big sister had completely abandoned them for a new family or a new home.

But for Siobhan, the contrast between Derry's Bogside and the rural idyll of Rose's home life surely could not have been more stark. I can see, however, she would have been determined not to allow the comparison to degrade the feelings she had of her own home. I wonder if those feelings explain why Siobhan asked Rose to spend time with her in Ireland the following summer—intending to show her friend an Ireland soft, verdant, and peopled even in the cities by warm, lyrical folk—people I know from the other side of my family. People with pride and love of country.

Jumping forward to summer, the story is well rehearsed. I got it from Mum and Dad at different times and often.

Mum had been immediately enthusiastic about the invitation and the prospect of experiencing the land a few miles off the coast from her home turf. Peggy was less positive, and her grandpa was highly vocal in his concern.

"Going over to Ireland right now isn't sensible. I can't see the trouble there going away any time soon. Make sure you don't go over around the 12th," he said, alluding to what the Ulstermen called, the marching season. The marches celebrate in a provocative, some would say violently aggressive way, the July anniversary of the 1690 Battle of the Boyne and the defeat of the Catholic King James.

Mum, with a sense of youthful invincibility, assured them Siobhan's mother was a sensible woman and would steer them away from any problems.

"We're going to go down to County Armagh to visit some of Siobhan's family who are in a folk band. We'll not be near Belfast, and we won't even be staying in Derry much, and I'll be home long before July the twelfth. The trouble-makers are in little pockets in the cities, and we won't be going anywhere near those places."

No one in Mum's family had heard of Derry's Bogside or the Rossville Flats as the nineteen sixties drew to a close. No one in

Dumfries was calling County Armagh, bandit country, at least not in their hearing. Not then. Siobhan and her family were, understandably in Rose's estimation, republicans with a small *r*. Up to that point, talk between the young women regarding Ireland, had been centred on academic discussions of literature, common history, and the oddity of Ulster, or the six counties as the republicans called them, in terms of civil and employment rights.

It was, however, impossible for anyone who lived in the Britain of the time to be unaware of growing political tensions. The nightly news broadcasts showed pitched battles in the streets, overturned buses in flames, the police and British Army fighting a losing battle on the streets.

Rose and Siobhan each in their own way, must have found a safe place to stand and I'm sure each could easily access their measure of innate remorse. For Rose it was the land-grab encouraged by a much earlier Scottish King, added to later by the actions of the Auxiliaries and the Black and Tans—mercenaries used to put down the uprisings in the early part of the century. For Siobhan it was the emerging violent muscle-flexing of the Provisional Irish Republican Army and the smell of burning tyres in the streets.

One night in front of the fire in Mum and Dad's living room, she told me a little gem about the time around graduation and how she had worried about Siobhan—how her evident liberal leanings, her love for the English language, would mean she would struggle to find a career in a place defined by prejudice and barriers, both real and virtual.

She added, "If only I knew then how much there was to worry about in her future."

I didn't pick this up when she first said it and had to wait until I could sit with her, face to face.

For herself, Mum hadn't decided on a personal career path but was firmly set against the option Peggy was promoting, the idea of following Henry into teaching. For the past two summers she'd volunteered twice weekly at Dumfries Museum. She'd managed to fit the shifts into her work commitments at the cafe-cum-gift shop owned by Mrs. McWhirter—an enterprising choir-lady from Germany who was married to a local farmer.

The job helped with the cost of her accommodation and living expenses in St. Andrews, and she purposefully kept in touch with the curator when she returned to St. Andrews, enthusing about his plans for the development of the small Burns Centre close to the banks of the River Nith.

"That's how you get a job. You use your contacts," she would remind me often.

In the Spring of her final year, she decided to step up her campaign, going from merely hinting at the future, to writing a letter declaring her interest in a job at the Centre. The curator advised her to volunteer for the summer and then to talk with them about the outlook at that point.

In the early summer, Mum graduated with BA(Hons) alongside Siobhan. Peggy, Walter, and the boys came to the ceremony and took both girls under their wing. Rose had booked a table for lunch in town and the family returned to Dumfries in the evening, leaving the young women to pack, return the gowns they had rented for the day and work their last days at their respective hotel jobs.

There are no pictures of Siobhan's family on that day. She'd discouraged her mother from even contemplating the expense.

"Waste of good money. All speeches and hanging around."

She'd promised them a framed picture and a celebratory meal out for the extended family when she arrived home.

But she was, as it turned out, going home with a concrete plan. With her strong interest in social planning, she'd won a place in a post-graduate programme at Glasgow University. And Mum said she chose to believe her wish to have her friend stay in Scotland was being looked on kindly from above.

The day after graduation, Mum and her two friends returned the key to the flat that had been their home during term time. Henry came to St Andrews to collect Rose, Siobhan and their mountain of bags and belongings.

The women were headed to Dumfries *en route* to Stranraer and the ferry to Larne.

I wonder how tense the overnight stay at the farm was. But I imagine Walter and Peggy put on a good show lest Siobhan take any reticence as a personal insult.

On the back of the photo dated the next day, it reads, "Me, Siobhan and Henry taking the ponies for a dawn trek before we set out for Larne."

Mum had described to me once when we were doing the same crossing, how Henry took charge of the driving and the luggage and how he had waved as she hung onto the rail, wind blowing across her face. She, no doubt, watched as the Irish coast crept into view before the coast of Scotland fully disappeared.

I was reminded of Henry's infatuation when I learned his last words as they parted company were to insist Siobhan keep writing to him. Mum never described this attachment as romantic. I can believe she might have been a bit selfish, not wanting to see them as a couple who might break up and leave her in an awkward spot. From her perspective, any momentary pining Henry might be doing was almost certainly better than a broken-hearted Henry, or perhaps worse, Henry the rogue who ruined her friend's happiness.

4. `Rose - Mary

Source: Conversation with Rose – mother
Time Reference: 1970

To get the really clear picture I'm after, I decided not to depend on my memory any further and travelled to Dumfries, and ask Rose, my mum to go right back to the first visit she made to Derry with Siobhan. I already had a sense of the fun they had and of how it cemented their relationship, but now I wanted to pin down how things changed between her and Siobhan—did the close attachment last? And when, if at all, did sit start to fade?

At the time I called her to say I wanted to visit, I hadn't been home for months, not since their thirty-fifth wedding anniversary party months before, the geography a metaphor for the emotional distance that currently lay between Mum and me. The distance had grown organically almost silently. There had been no family row or perceived slight on my part. The only flashpoint happened last Christmas when I hinted she was not confronting the possibility that something in Siobhan's Irish past could have led to her murder. I'd had a couple of beers at the party, and she ignored me, and took food through to the sitting room. That, no doubt, explained her end of the distance-keeping.

Mum's opinion remained that Siobhan's death could only have been the result of a random shooting on a seashore in Canada. This theory seemed so improbable to me, inviting frustration and lately, anger. However, perhaps because she was used to her son story writing, and of his interest in Bloody Sunday and the Saville Enquiry, and probably believing there was no harm because I was on the road to nowhere, she agreed to give me time and I travelled down the following weekend.

I wanted to hear her talk one-on-one in the red sandstone house I grew up in. I was gambling I'd get tougher and be more probing than I had been to date. She'd be at ease on her own territory.

So the thinking went.

On Saturday, my mother, whom I think of as ageless, sat at the family dining table. Her figure was trim like the girl in the photos, greyness kept in check with mahogany hair dye. She was

56

wearing slacks—never jeans. She liked lamb's wool sweaters and oversized cashmere scarves. I have never seen her wear jewellery apart from her engagement and wedding rings.

Regardless of her agreement to answer my questions, I noticed signs of what I took to be irritation as we moved to settle down—the rough handling of the cutlery drawer, the bang with which the coffee mug was put down in front of me, the tutting when the phone rang as we were about to get started. Experience had taught me I was not meant to ask if anything was the matter when she was like this. It was Mum's form of passive aggression and had to be allowed its outlet. I played along by sitting still and leaning forward neutrally to show attention to whatever she would choose to say when she sat down.

As she talked, she kept an eye on both the cooker timer and the nickel-coloured recorder I'd placed in front of her. From time to time, she used the hem of her apron to scour away a finger mark on the polished wooden surface.

Even at the start, her eyes were moist, but no tears escaped.

She opened with the events that bridged the story from Dumfries to Derry.

```
TRANSCRIPT - CONVERSATION WITH ROSE

I remember almost everything about my
first trip to Ireland, like, Siobhan
saying when we took the bus to take us
from Larne to the City, "Thank God I
```

sent those boxes with my books and stuff on earlier."

Yeah, thank God. We'd got it down to two bags and a rucksack each, but even then, the dour driver acted like it was a personal affront for anyone to arrive from the ferry with so much stuff in tow.

Then, we got a black taxi out to the Bogside. Siobhan chose the cab, knowing the ones that would go into her territory. I was learning how things worked as I went along.

We rounded a corner where a local artist had painted a mural stating, 'You are Entering Free Derry.' And suddenly we were at the Rossville Flats. Exhausted. We unloaded the bags on the pavement outside the very latest thing in city-planning.

[I checked Mum's face because I wasn't quite used to the sarcastic tone coming out of her mouth. It took my curiosity up a level. She went on without meeting my eye.]

I took it all in, quickly. Kids lolling about, standing on top of beer cans and rubble, faces hidden by broad, red kerchiefs, no grass, no playground, bare. And then there were the three big blocks of flats built mostly with glass

set into multi-coloured cement blocks.
I took in the whole scene which fairly
shouted a mix of decay and violence.
And I don't mind admitting I wondered
if I'd been a bit naïve about safety.

[Note: I wanted to check in and asked, "Anything else about your impressions of the neighbourhood—the buildings the gangs?"]

I can close my eyes and see those coloured blocks. I felt like they were
desperately trying and failing to bring
a bit of cheer to the neighbourhood.
From that moment on it was clear to me
where Siobhan's got her interest in social planning. I never questioned it
again.
Siobhan's mother, Mary, came out to
greet us. She'd obviously been watching
at the front room window. I guessed,
watching the action below was a hobby
for the women there. She started speaking right away. Fast. Irish. Northern.

[Note: Mum either consciously or unconsciously, slipped into her imitation of the accent and she occasionally gig-gled in the retelling.]

"For the love of God come away in you
two. You must be parched. I've the kettle

59

on and some scones fresh this morning
from Timmy's. Put those bags down on the
floor. Aidan! Get these bags up to our
Siobhan's room."
And as soon as Aiden showed his head
around the doorway Siobhan attacked him
with a hug. He pinked-up with embarrass-
ment.
He shoved her off and hitched up his
jeans. "Get off or I'll never manage to
get this stuff out of the way."
With a two-handed grip, he took the first
bag along the corridor. I thought of your
uncle Thomas and his snake-hips. I suspected both five-five to five six in
height.
Siobhan got down to the formal introduc-
tions.

*[Note: Mum looked straight into my face, bringing the
scene closer, blocking any outside distractions. Dad was
somewhere else in the house. I could hear his footfall
above. She was recreating the scene for me in as much
detail as she could remember. Happy days.]*

"Ma, this is the Rose you've heard so
much about. Rose, that's Aidan you've
just met. Where's Brendan?" I handed Mary
the bag containing jams and vegetables,
packed fresh when I'd left home that
morning.

I was gob-smacked by how Mary was so ca-
pable at handling two topics at the same
time.

"He's out, probably at his girlfriend's
place. He says he'll see you both later."
And without a breath, "Look at all the
stuff. Rose, you need to thank your
mother for sending this. Now, come away
in an' tell me all your latest news.
There's the kettle boiling, sit yourselves down, grab a plate and tuck in."
Siobhan and her mother chatted about
cousins, aunts, grandfathers, neighbours, Aidan's schooling, and Brendan's
lack of luck in finding work. I remember
the talk was full of coded phrases like:
"he's in the usual trouble," "the one who
had to leave in a hurry," and "she's an
awful worry to her family."

Mary bobbed around the kitchen and took
tea and goodies to Aidan who'd settled
into watching the TV. I was working hard
to keep up with the banter. After four
years I'd no trouble with Siobhan's accent but the quick-fire rounds of Derry-
talk was another thing all together.

When the conversation lulled. Mary sat
down and turned to me.

"Siobhan tells me you likely have a job
to go to. I think it's great you know so
much about yer fella Burns. He's a great
way with words, for sure."

It must have been about this time the subject of the next-door neighbour came up. Not that she was really important but I'm trying to tell you what it was like in the house. It heaved with the kind of energy I wasn't used to. Warm but chaotic. The kind that said, 'you're welcome but you need to take us as you find us.' Then Mary said something like, go next-door and ask old Mrs. Collins to come in for a cuppa tea. She's on her own and so I have her over most days. I've left it a bit late today so she could have a bit of a chat with you two, but we'll mind not to let her stay too long. The Good Lord knows, she'd spend the night here if we didn't pay attention."

Siobhan returned with a grey-haired lady, dressed in pink and blue, who'd brought her knitting along. We all went to the living room, forcing Aidan out of his seat and the house. I noticed Aidan came and went without much accounting. So different to the way the whereabouts of your uncle Thomas was known to my parents at all times.

Mrs. Collins, got down to business. "You'll be the one with the horses and the farm." And switching subjects without blinking, "Do you know any Scottish songs you could give us?"

"I'm not much of a singer." She'd caught me on the hop—not used to being asked to sing in the homes of virtual strangers.

"Nonsense," said Siobhan, smiling slyly and being careful not to specify which church, "Sure, she's sung in the church for years."

After a lot of coaxing, red faced, I took the safe route of the Burn's song, Annie Laurie.

The old lady took my singing as the cue to start her own repertoire. She occasionally paused to lubricate her throat with tea. She hinted that Irish whiskey was the very best thing to keep a singer's throat in good condition but was ignored by Mary who used her eyes to signal Siobhan shouldn't start to ply her with drink.

After an hour or so, Siobhan's mother, no doubt with plenty of practice in keeping these visits under control said, "Let's hear, Carrickfergus from you Mrs. Collins and then I have to get these young ladies sorted out."

With no need of further encouragement, the old lady tipped back the remains of her tea and began:

I wish I were in Carrickfergus,
Only for nights in Ballygrand...

At the end, there was applause which included Brendan and Aidan who'd joined us
midway through the first verse.
I have such a clear memory of Brendan
making the courtly offer to Mrs. Collins
of the crook of his arm.
"Let me walk you home, Mrs. Collins."
"Now young man, don't you be looking to
lead me astray. I hear about you and your
way with the girls."
Brendan led her out, being careful to
collect her knitting lest she have an
excuse to come back at some time later
in the evening. Over his shoulder he
mouthed, "I'll be back in a tick."
When he returned, he said his formal
hello to me and took his sister for a
whirl around the room asking, "What's for
tea Ma?"
Mary didn't answer him directly.
"Jesus, Mary and Joseph I thought she was
here for the duration. Well done, Brendan. I'm putting a pie in the oven and
the potatoes on to boil. It should be
half an hour. You girls can freshen up."

*[Note: I butted in. "What did Brendan look like back
then?"]*

He was a bit flabby, dressed in the usual
jeans and a tee shirt—but up to the minute, you know. His hair was longish and

wavy. I could see how he'd have appealed to women. He could fix you with a gaze and a smile.

Anyway, Siobhan led the way upstairs before we ate, and we discussed the sleeping and washing arrangements.

"We'll need to share the bed. I hope you don't mind?"

"Not at all. But don't snore or remember I'll be close enough to smother you with a pillow."

We lay side by side on top of the covers and I said something like, "I love the talent your mother has to string the names of the divine and saints together when she gets excited. It's a gift. My favourite from today was, 'Jesus, Mary and Joseph, St. Patrick and all the saints, would you turn down that telly, Aidan.' Now I know how many saints it takes to turn down a TV. The answer is— all of them."

And then I remember the mood changing in the room, probably because I said, "I've never asked before, how did your father die?"

Now, she knew almost everything about my life story and me not very much about hers. I must've thought it was about time for that to change but, at the same time, we were on her turf. We weren't in St. Andrews or Dumfries anymore. I was quite

ready for some story of sectarian violence if that what was coming.

Siobhan continued, "I thought I'd told
you already, it was lung cancer. He was
diagnosed a year after Aidan was born and
dead eight months later. I think that's
why I fuss and worry over the boy as
much. It was hard to lose his dad when
he was so young."

I'd never thought her concern about Aidan
excessive, but Siobhan went on explaining, and it helped me make sense of the
plan for the next few days.

"It's hard in these parts to grow up
without a father. Brendan's around, but
he's not much to look up to. Fun, but not
exactly the role model I'd pick."

She looked at me directly. "I hope you
don't mind about taking Aidan to the
cousin's farm with us. I thought it was
a great chance to get him away for a
while and he'll have the company of my
Cousin Fergal's kids."

"No problem at all. He seems a really
nice lad. Do you think he's got it in him
to go to college or university?" Even
though I'd only just met him, I wanted
to see a path for him out of the social
depravation I'd seen on the street.

Siobhan was emphatic. "He will if I've
anything to do with it. That's another
reason for me to get him away with us to

66

the farm so we can talk. He's young yet but boys can grow up too fast around here and end up in trouble before you know it."

Actually, I was pleased about taking this on with her because it was testimony to how close we had become.

"It'll be fun to have him along," I said. "Don't forget, I'm used to the company of males."

I suspect because we'd got to a comfortable spot in the conversation, she took the chance to ask me a personal question. She asked me about my biological father and if it was possible that I really didn't know who he was.

I wanted to shut the subject down as quickly as I could and said, "No, I don't, and I've never asked. I picked up somewhere his name was Robert but nothing much else. You know I wouldn't ever want to pry and risk upsetting my mum and I'd never insult my father by picking away at the past. Walter's always taken care of me. I've never known any different and I wouldn't trade him in for any man alive."

Siobhan pushed me a bit more. "But really, you're not even a wee bit curious about where he came from, where he went, what he looks like?"

"Nope, not even a little bit.

[Note: Mum paused to look at me her dark eyes wide, as if she knew I'd learned more about her early days via my dad, and demanding in that look, that I keep her confidence. She added the next piece, looking at me directly— 'That's as true now as it was then.' Something else jumped out at me, that the visit and the conversations with Siobhan must have left Mum in no doubt about the dangers of living in Derry, of how easily people could be drawn into violence and crime. So hard for Mum to ignore then or deny later.

Mum went on with the story.]

Now, Siobhan didn't give up easily. "You kill me Rose, I would never have been able to control my curiosity all these years. I'd have plagued my Ma with questions until I got the low-down on the guy."

I don't remember anything else being said on the subject and baths became the priority. If nothing else, it got me out of the hot seat.

And the next morning was warm and humid. I lay wondering, because the heat had already built up within the thin walls, how they could possibly protect against winter's weather. I thought of the great protective granite of the farmhouse and of my good fortune.

We had a satisfying breakfast, toast and eggs, before we set off to see the walls of the Old City of Derry. We meandered, window-shopped, and shared a bag of chips as we walked, nothing remarkable, and we arrived back in time for tea with Aunt Brigit, Mary's older sister. Aidan seemed to be waiting for us as we pulled up in a taxi. He yelled over his shoulder "See ya," to the boys he'd been with.

We found Aunt Brigit and Mary in the kitchen cutting up ham, ready to serve the cabbage and potatoes that were part of yesterday's gift bag from the farm.

Come the evening, we had a few drinks, and the singing broke out again. Brigit had a big repertoire of American country and western songs. I never have figured out the connection between that music and Derry.

Siobhan insisted her mother sang, *The Wind that Shakes the Barley.* I remembered the poem from a student assignment Siobhan wrote way back in our second year. The sound of it put to music made me teary. I tried to keep my head down until Brendan rolled in around eleven. I can still picture it. His mother slapped him hard on the arm as he started on a chorus of *The Bold Fenian Men,* very partisan, and Mary jumped on it.

"You watch yourself. Our Siobhan has her friend staying. And while I'm on the subject, you make sure people about here know Rose is a university pal of our Siobhan's. I don't want any unpleasantness.

I got the idea. I was in Catholic Derry and needed at least low-grade protection.

Brendan started on 'Bridge Over Troubled Water' and at some time, Aidan phoned for a taxi to collect his Aunt Brigit. I began to wonder if I had the stamina to keep up with that level of socialising for days on end, but I wasn't going to be the party pooper. I owed it to Siobhan to join in.

[I had a question. "Seems like a bit of a change of pace for you. Did you enjoy it?"

Mum hardly broke her stride.

"You know, I thought of it like part of a rite of passage. I was on holiday, away from home, no parents—so of course I enjoyed it. But the best was yet to come, so be patient."

I knew what she was alluding to, a time of innocence when she found her true love, and before things were for ever corrupted. She checked her watch and then she looked at me through her eyelashes, not shy, more secretive. She continued talking.]

The next evening had been booked for the family celebration of Siobhan's graduation. And for this, Aunt Brigit, her two daughters, and Siobhan's late father's brother Jimmy, joined the party at a hotel somewhere on the edge of the city. Siobhan made a fuss of presenting her mother with a framed picture of herself in full graduation regalia and gave over her scroll to be put away for safe keeping. We showed our stack of graduation day pictures around. Brendan grabbed one of the snaps and asked when he could get an introduction to Pamela. Siobhan punched his arm, telling him it would likely be the day after he graduated from Cambridge and somehow came by a large fortune.

Mary added, "You make sure you take these with you to show your Uncle Paddy and the cousins on the farm. They'll love to get a look at them."

[Note: I felt I had to ask, to make sure I was getting the mood and atmosphere correct. "So, you're among all her relatives, everything's all sweetness and Irish charm, and none of them make a big thing of you being a Scot or a Protestant? Was there no tension? Nothing?
"I'm telling you exactly as it was. Her family couldn't have been more welcoming. Now let me get onto this next bit before we eat lunch."]

The next morning, Sunday, I came downstairs, and everyone was getting ready for Mass. I asked outright if I could go with them. I didn't want to sit around on my own and I don't mind admitting, I was a bit curious.

Without turning a hair Mary said, "That would be grand if you'd like to." If she even hesitated, I didn't notice.

Siobhan whispered to me, "You don't need to. I'm only going because it makes Ma happy."

"It's okay, I want to. You came to church with my family at Christmas. Besides, I've never been inside a Catholic church."

Mary was constantly in motion but overheard and said, "Well, we need to get going or you won't be seeing the inside of this one either."

It turned out her judgement had been on the money. Our group, including Aidan and Brendan, walked to the church and managed to slip into the few remaining places in chairs lined up against the back wall to take the overspill from the pews. I heard soft coughing and watched people shifting around to let others cram into the last seats. After the hymns, the bells, the priest and the altar boys, thirty minutes, and it was over.

At the end, Mary took me firmly by the arm and forced me through the crowd of men who had been standing outside of the church. Siobhan let me know later these were the lads who would swear to their mothers they'd been to morning Mass, even though they hadn't put a foot inside the church. They couldn't even claim to be able to hear anything of the service from outside. But no doubt, as far as they were concerned, their duty of attendance had been met.

Mary picked up the pace, nodding occasionally to friends but not stopping to make conversation or, more particularly, to answer potential enquiries about me, her visitor.

She herded us like a collie. "For the love of the saints, I'm dying for a cup of tea and some breakfast. Let's get home." We followed at a trot. To the outside eye and those of the plain clothes police on the other side of the street, we must have looked like the personification of the perfect Catholic family returning from their devotions.

The rest of day was only broken by Mrs. Collins coming by for tea, and a few verses of 'The Irish Rover.'

[Note: I sensed Mum was ready to take a breather. She glanced over the table at me to emphasise an important point for me to take on board.

She spoke to me looking directly into my eyes: "So you see, it was very pleasant. All of them behaved perfectly as far as I was concerned. I was having a good time and I thought they were great—different from my family but still great. I'll go to my grave saying no one gave a damn about my religion and they didn't ask one question about my views on the trouble going on."

I asked, "Is there a chance it was because they were being polite for Siobhan's sake? I suspect people over there might have become expert at skirting around difficult subjects and putting a good face on things?"

Mum eyes flared, for a second. "What things?"

"Do I really need to answer that? And besides, maybe they wouldn't want to embarrass Siobhan?"

Mum was on her guard. "I don't want you reading anything more into this story than there really was. And they weren't the kind of people who could hide their feelings. They were kind, natural. You could take them at face value."

"Duly noted," I said.

"Let's see what your dad has to say about it when he comes down. In the meantime, I'll finish this bit of the story and I'll get lunch served up."

She took up where she left off.]

The next morning, I said my thanks to Mary after I'd finished packing. She tried to persuade me to come back with Siobhan after we'd been to the farm. I explained how much I'd love to but needed to get home because of my summer job and the museum waiting for me.

74

But I did say, "I'd love to come back again some other time."

Siobhan, Aidan, Mary, and I went down to the car Brendan had borrowed from a friend. Aidan packed our gear into the back, and we set off, waving until Mary was out of sight.

I remember Brendan giving out brotherly advice, but not before taking care of a bit of business.

"Now, you tell that miserable sod of a Cousin Fergal, he still owes me twenty quid from the time he last visited. And don't let those country eegits give you any trouble. And if you go over the border keep an eye out for the army patrols on this side. They're watching the border crossings. If they stop you, don't give them any reason to turn nasty. And don't smuggle any contraception over the border."

I thought it was funny in the way sisters understand how it was to get advice from older brothers—different circumstances, different advice—but the spirit of it was exactly the same.

Siobhan gave him short change. "Anything else? You mind and keep yourself out of mischief. We're going to be with the family. They know their way around. We'll have fun and won't be provoking any soldiers."

Brendan stood down but couldn't seem to resist having the last word.

"You watch all the same. And when the train gets to Belfast, don't leave the station. Just change onto the next train going south. You don't know any people there. Phone me if you need anything. Jesus, I think I liked it better when you were in Scotland."

"Well, you'll only have to worry about me for a few weeks and I'll be off again. Now give me a hug so I can get rid of you."

As we watched Brendan walk off toward the car, Siobhan sighed. "I wish he was settled in a job. Being on the dole's no life for a young man."

I was conscious of the police, armed, not like the mainland. A few soldiers standing around in small groups with their coal black rifles slung from their shoulders gave me the heebie-jeebies. And then a driver suddenly slammed the back door of a newspaper delivery van behind us. I remember it because I felt like I leapt ten feet in the air. Siobhan grabbed my arm. She said she felt guilty because she hadn't thought of the impact the place would have on the uninitiated.

I was relieved when the engine pulled into the station, and we could get on board. As we sat, waiting for the train to pull out the soldiers walked up and down the platform, looking in the windows with unveiled suspicion at the seated passengers.

"Are they looking for somebody?" I asked Siobhan.

"You never can tell, and you certainly never ask them."

The train lurched forward, and I don't remember much else. We chugged along on the four-hour journey to the farm in Ulster's southeast.

END OF TRANSCRIPT

Mum got up to check the oven.

"Give your dad a shout. We should eat. And anyway, it would be a good idea for him to be here for the next bit. Don't you think?"

5. The Patricks and Connor

Source: Conversation with Rose, mother, with contributions from Connor, father
Time Reference: 1970

Mum's habit of feeding me as if war was about to be declared persisted into my adulthood. The table was cleared of my accoutrements and laid by Mum for the three of us to eat. The afternoon sun was shining in and Mum pulled down the blinds. They snapped down unevenly and she exhaled loudly when she had to straighten them. She took the chance to open the windows a peep. I could hear the rumbling of the traffic passing to and from Dalbeattie. I remembered sitting on the ledge as a kid waving to the people who passed on foot. I plunked myself down and drew up my stocking-soled feet to sit sideways and reminisce.

It didn't take long for Dad to call me to the table. I looked at him from my perch. His once dark curls were now silver. He'd put on a little weight around the middle, but his face was unlined, and I silently hoped I'd inherited his genes. Although it has to be said he kept himself a lot tidier and well put together than me.

As we sat down, I asked if I could use the recorder as we talked and ate so I didn't need to take notes. They looked at each other. An understanding, in a code I was never privy to, was silently signalled between them, and Dad said, "You do what you need to get this business out of your system."

There it was, a few words making it clear they had little or no motivation to pursue the story. In other words, they were humouring me—presumably hoping I would either lose interest or would not have the journalistic chops to do a thorough job. The hole in the toe of my socks and my need of a haircut was probably enough to confirm their suspicion I hadn't quite matured enough to be the kind of professional I fancied myself to be. They were taking me no more seriously than back when I was working on a high school project. If I had been trying to go undercover, I'd have to say it worked, but this wasn't a furtive move, I'm a natural slob.

I watched Dad while he settled the mashed potatoes on a cork mat in the centre of the table. I was looking for signs of annoyance not detectable in his voice, but there were none. My own look was probably hard to read, but he didn't make a comment, and I had neither the need nor desire to go off on some tangent about my motivation. I chose to take the gift of time graciously and shut up about anything else for the time being.

The anticipation of the meal made my mouth water—I used to say 'made my mouth sweat' when I was a child sitting at the same table, waiting for our meal to be served. There it was, the remembered sweet smell of honeyed ham, and carrots from my grandparent's farm. I was back in the warm wrap of home.

I'd been hungrier than I thought, and when almost sated, I relaxed enough to join in the talk, but still the conversation mostly rattled between my parents. Any intrusion on my part as the story was told was largely unneeded, each of them filled in bits and pieces of detail the other was in danger of forgetting or had raced over. We'd reached the point of the story they loved to tell, their love story. For the most part, I knew I could let them run with it, only occasionally feeling the need to intervene and make sure I hadn't missed a precious detail about Siobhan.

Getting to Newry in the story helped me colour in details about many of the characters. The country relatives, as I always called them, had a rustic Emerald Isle persona I'd known all my life, but I listened for any gems, any signs of family stress. I could visualise Siobhan and Aiden with softer edges acquired as they melted into the farm on the outskirts of the town and were distanced from the streets of Derry.

And in my opinion, this was the point in time Rose, my mother, broke from her girlhood, became a whole mature person embarking on an independent path. As I tap the keys, adding notes as needed to the transcript of the recording, she slowly becomes the Mum, the person I know.

NOTES FROM LUNCH TIME CONVERSATION -
ROSE AND CONNOR

Rose: I remember arriving at the farm
in a slightly rusty Ford van driven by
Patrick, Siobhan's cousin. In spite of
the fact, he stood over six feet tall,
I learned he was always called Wee Patrick.
The landscape reminded me of home but
the farmhouse itself was completely
different to the one I knew in Dumfries. This house was low-slung, suffering from fading whitewash probably
applied decades ago. The barns were unkempt. Hens pecked at the ground, a
cockerel strutted, and a few ducks
roamed freely.

*[Note: reference a photo—the property had the mien of
the House that Jack Built —a bit added on here and there
with no obvious plan.]*

Rose: Wee Patrick led us through to the
large kitchen. Heat met us at the door,
generated by a large stove, the only
apparent means of cooking. He placed
the large kettle on the range and
shouted for his mother, "Mammy, our

Siobhan and Aidan are here. Where are you?"

"I'm right here," Mammy replied emerging from some deep part of the building.

Explaining for us visitors that her husband, Old Paddy, had the flu, had taken to his bed, and was keeping her on the hop with his demands for hot toddies and lemon cold remedies.

Connor: This was in the middle of the summer, mind.

Rose: I remember an indistinct cry coming from the dark recesses of the cottage and Mammy yelling, "For the love of God and all the saints, will you give me a minute, and then to Wee Patrick, "Go see what he wants now. Sit down the rest of you and I'll get you some supper. It's ready in the oven."

With the extolling of God and the saints, the sisterhood of Mammy here and Mary in Derry had been established for all time in my mind.

Connor: My mam, their other sister, was cut from the same cloth.

Rose: After Wee Patrick had attended to the need of his ailing father, we settled down to dinner, joined by Brother Paddy who was Mammy's brother and who came daily to help around the farm. He nodded his welcome to all and spoke not one word until his plate was cleared. Then he thanked Mammy for the meal and let them know he'd see them in the morning, adding he'd get here for the milking so Old Paddy didn't need to stir from his sick bed.

[Note: I got my mum to pause for a minute while I got a pen out of my satchel and penned some points in my notebook. I wanted to take care. These were Dad's people, and he would never allow me to portray them as Irish caricatures, with saints, and shamrock, and the little people (the temptation would be strong.) I'd travelled there several times as a schoolboy. Dad once told me their lifestyle was dying. It was too hard-scrabble a life to exist long into the twenty-first century. But they were proud of the farm, and of how it had given them independence. And the land, oh the land, a security hard won, literally blood stained. They and their neighbours had fought for the right to own land rather than be driven off. There were ancestors who had died of hunger and were buried there, forgotten in all but myth, graves unmarked.
They were Siobhan's people, Aidan's people, and my people.
I nodded at Mum to go on]

Rose: After the meal, we were shown to our rooms. Aidan was put in the room under the roof and us young women in a room at the end of the hall beside Wee Patrick. There were clean sheets, and we were told the water was good and hot for a wash or a bath.

I remember how we sank down on the beds, and how I'd said, "I hope I can keep straight all the Patricks in the house."

Siobhan replied, "There's certainly a lack of imagination around naming the boys. Still, it saves a bit on the old memory. Just yell Patrick and someone's bound to show up."

She then set about finding her soap bag and saying she would take the bathroom first if it was okay.

Aidan had wandered into the room as Siobhan was singing in the bathroom.

[Note: In the telling, Mum seemed to be transported back there—she was looking over my shoulder, never directly at me. I didn't interrupt because I knew it was important to allow her to recall the scene in detail, to be clear about the forces at work and how things fell into place and helped to draw her in.]

Rose: I remember Aiden saying the room he was to sleep in was like an oven and he asked if we could have a game of cards or something? Explaining, "They've no telly here."

85

He sat on the bed and produced cards from his pocket.

We played twenty-ones and joked about a bit, and I thought how much he was like my brother Thomas.

I said to him at some point, "I hear some of your cousins are coming over later. You'll be glad to see them?"

And he replied, "Yeah, Cousin Fergal has a boy of fifteen, like me, he's called Paddy-boy around the family. And there's a girl called Marie, about twelve I reckon. I hear from Uncle Wee Patrick us boys are to help with the hay tomorrow.

Aidan said he usually got paid for the help and how he was not going to spend it all on sweets and comics but planned to save some to get one of those cassette-players.

When Siobhan walked in towel-drying her hair she had asked, "Who's fleecing who?"

Aidan blurted out. "We were just joking around."

I recalled Siobhan's next words. They became imprinted in my mind.

"Rose don't you encourage him to gamble. I have plans for this young man. He's going to be a doctor not a card-shark."

Rose: I remember Aidan's self-deprecating reply. "Some hopes of me being a doctor. I've no brain for science or anything else." He had become red in the face and nudged his sister with his hip in a silent plea to shut up.
Sometime shortly after, there was a commotion in the hall. Fergal's clan had arrived.
Aidan rolled off the bed and got to his feet with a spring, folding his hand— two Kings.
I joined the people in the kitchen after a bath myself, and Siobhan introduced everyone.

[Note: The next part of the story telling comes from Mum and Dad jumping in and supplementing each other's recall. The story started to flow, and I resisted the urge to interrupt with questions. Mum started. Dad hadn't arrived on the scene at the beginning.]

Rose: The room was crowded—Wee Patrick and Fergal examined a bodhran, that's a traditional Irish hand-held drum and each took a turn in beating out a rhythm as they tapped their foot. They stopped for a bit but continued talking to each other.

"Young O'Dowd turns out a fine instrument."

They brought down the volume while listening to Siobhan talk about her graduation.

Mammy bustled around to make the entire company tea. The reverence to Old Patrick's care went on.

Mum remembered how she had leaned against the doorway, watching and listening as the conversation flashed around the room.

"Wee Patrick, will you check on your da in the bedroom back there. See if he needs anything."

"I took him a toddy not more than ten minutes ago. He says he won't be getting up but anyone who wants to can go through and see him."

Fergal offered to go along to the room in a minute or two.

At some point, the brothers produced a fiddle, and they gave the bodhran a good try-out. Surveying the happy disorder as I leaned against the wall, I realised how quiet my life at home seemed by comparison, and wondered how much Siobhan must have missed the clamour while she stayed in St. Andrews or at my family's place.

[Note: On one of my visits, I remember meeting Old Patrick, sometimes called The Chief, my dad's uncle. I was young and wearing my school uniform, that probably meant it was some family funeral or other. He was a small, stooped man. This was in contrast to what I was hearing of him lording over it in this scene.]

Connor: No doubt the craic went on all evening. That was the way of the place.
Rose: After tea and cake was served, Siobhan and I insisted Mammy sit down while we cleared the table and attended to the washing up. Wee Patrick joined us at the sink as Fergal went to visit with his father.
He asked if they were ready to go to Dundalk the next day—to the date the band had booked at Neil's Bar. He let us know they would head over the border in the daylight, play the gig, stay with Neil overnight and come back early the next afternoon. He added Connor and Maxine planned to come over to the farm

around noon and help them pack up their gear.

I remember Siobhan had specifically asked about someone called Michael O'Rourke.

The reply had been, "He's not doing any gigs right now—in a bit of trouble with one of the wild boyos—keeping his head down."

Siobhan had answered, "Too bad, you'll be missing his flute playing."

Wee Patrick had only commented they'd get by and how it was less to share the money with.

When the women eventually got to their room at the end of the evening, I had a list of questions:

"Who are Connor and Maxine?" – answer, cousins who play in the band.

"Why is Dundalk called Dodge City?" – answer, because it's a border town, on the Republic side. It has a bit of a wild reputation.

"What is a boyo?" – answer, a member of the Provisional IRA.

Mum had continued, "Is this Neil's Bar safe?"

Siobhan patiently reassured me, "We'll be fine. It's a popular music venue. Stay close to the band and don't ask anyone any questions."

Finally, I asked, "Will it be okay to sleep at this Neil's place when we don't know him."

Siobhan assured me she knew Neil and had said this was a chance for her to experience a bit of local colour: how Neil was a bit of a celebrity, had been in the IRA—in the Republic where it's a banned organisation, how he'd ended up in Dublin's Mountjoy Gaol for a couple of years. Siobhan said she didn't know what he'd done, so not to bother asking her; and when they demolished the building a few years back, he'd bought his cell door and made it the door to his bar.

I recall saying, "God Siobhan, you really have a whole other life I've never even guessed at."

And Siobhan had said, "It's not at all strange to me, nearly everyone in Ireland knows someone who's had an interesting past. Personally, I try to avoid the people who have an interesting present. So, relax. We're going to listen to the best in traditional Irish music and have some fun with the family."

[Note: I tentatively interrupted, asking, 'It seemed a message about where Siobhan stood in terms of what was going on in her homeland.'

Dad—'Yes it was. Very clear.'
Mum looked at him, not at me. The message signalled,
'we're together on this.'
I felt shut out. I looked from one to the other. Neither
took the bait]

[Note: I scribbled the next, jotting down fast so I didn't
forget.
Mum painted a clear picture of what she learned on the
trip, not only about local colour but about how the day-
to-day living in Ireland incorporated elements unknown
on mainland Britain: bands with members who could not
travel because of a falling out with local terrorists; men
who fixed cars or milked cows by day took shots at British
troops by night and then went to their children's school
concerts at Christmas; women whose warnings to their
sons to be careful had a whole different undertone. From
her vantage point she said she sensed a weird depravity
but which somehow lacked wickedness.
And she had solid comfort behind her. For all this was an
exercise in cognitive dissonance, Mum knew she would
be back on the ferry back to Stranraer soon enough and
could give it some perspective.]

Connor: The next day, I drove into the
yard in a Peugeot.
Rose: I thought he was the most handsome man I'd ever seen in the flesh.
Now, look at him blushing.

Back then, his hair was dark and curly, medium height, medium build with medium brown eyes, but I saw nothing of the medium about him. He could've played the role of the handsome gypsy in films. And I'd been relieved when I remembered Maxine, a gorgeous looking brunette who had arrived with him, was his sister.

And you know, Siobhan immediately noticed the force flashing between us as we were introduced. She told me later, in a conspiratorial whisper as we piled into the van for the journey south. "He's a catch. Teaches history and geography in Newry, and plays guitar and fiddle. If he wasn't my cousin, I'd be prepared to fight you for him."

[Note: Dad, who loved to spin a good yarn, slipped into his troubadour mode at this point. But Mum continued to interject. I noticed I relaxed more when he spoke, in contrast to when Mum was speaking and I felt on edge—eager not to miss a detail, a beat or the nuance of how she said something.]

Connor: With being crammed in among the musical instruments and the general overcrowding in the van, the journey was uncomfortable but fortunately short. Of course, we were stopped at a checkpoint on the Armagh side of the border by British soldiers, all jittery in camouflage gear. The three privates looked to be in their early twenties and were accompanied by a senior member of the platoon. He stood back and wrote down the number of their vehicle licence plate. Wee Patrick, the driver, was asked for the groups' destination and we were sent on our way. Everyone inside the van stayed silent until we were waved through. No one disturbed the peace or made comments. We exhaled and drove on—business as usual in the Northern Ireland of the time.

The border crossing on the Republic side, was manned by a cliché of a man, lone, fat, bearded, dressed in an ill-fitting green uniform. He asked Wee Patrick what he had on board and received confirmation the intention was not to sell the instruments.

"Jesus, I hope it doesn't come to that," Wee Patrick had said biting the inside of his mouth to stop himself laughing.

Then, an unremarked man cycled over the border with a bag slung under his cross bar. For all anyone knew or seemed to care, the bag might have contained a side of meat, a bomb, or carpenter's

94

tools. The guard didn't bat an eyelid as the man rode onwards to the distant hills of County Louth. I assumed he must have been a regular the guard knew, and after the tense experience at the army checkpoint, this incident seemed almost farcical. I asked your mum at the time why she was laughing. "Tension I expect," she said.

We found a place to eat, crowded around a large table in the middle of a cafe selling soup, sandwiches, and a variety of pies. What passed for air conditioning was the door, left open to let the steam out and the heat in. I barely noticed the temperature and lack of breathable air as the conversation centred on the band confirming their set for the night.

In the typical family chaos of duelling conversations, Siobhan showed Maxine the pictures she had brought from St. Andrews. We asked for a photo to take home. I picked one with Rose and Siobhan standing together outside of the graduation hall.

Rose: I wish I hadn't been squinting so much when it was taken.

Connor: After the meal, we walked out to the edge of the sea and along a path following the high-water mark. I fell

into step with Mum and Siobhan who
linked arms.

"How long are you staying for, Rose?"
I asked.

She said, "I go back to Scotland when
we leave here on Friday. Siobhan and I
will travel to Belfast together then
I'll catch a train to Larne. I need to
be back for work on Monday."

I saw my chance to get to know her better. "You'll get a chance to look
around a bit then. Siobhan, won't you
bring her over to meet my mam before
you leave?"

"Sounds like a good idea," Siobhan
said. It was a fun, a light-hearted
scene, and I moved on to ambush Fergal
from behind. The ensuing friendly wres-
tling left both of us a bit wet. Maxine
warned them not to come near her because she'd nothing to change into.

At seven o'clock we pulled up in front
of Neil's Pub.

*[Note: He stopped, and Mum seemed eager to take over.
I paused and opened the window wider, fearing a sweat
coming, and I was wearing a light shirt that would show
under-arm damp patches.]*

Rose: I remember the warning issued.
"Now," said Wee Patrick, "Make sure

folk know Rose is Scottish. We wouldn't want anyone mistaking her for English," and him turning to me saying, "Don't worry you'll be fine."

We all climbed a short flight of stairs and Connor knocked on the door. I assumed the place must still be closed, but then there was a noise from inside as the person on the other side slid the lock. I assumed the locked-door routine was some form of extreme security measure or crowd management.

Connor: I knew she'd be worried, so I whispered in her ear, "It's to keep out the undesirables."

Rose: I wondered at the time what that was code for.

Connor: The usual cheer went up from the patrons as we trailed through the smoky room.

Rose: As the band got set up on the stage, I had a chance to look around the walls. After realising exactly what I was looking at, I tried not to stare. There were as many as thirty photos depicting people who had been, as the banner said, 'Killed in the Struggle for Freedom', each picture was draped by the crossed green, white, and gold flags of the Republic. I decided in an instant to stay close to Siobhan. For the rest of the evening we sat, went to the bathroom, and conversed in tandem.

I asked about the photos on the walls when I was sitting with Siobhan and Connor before the band went on stage. Your dad had been the one to explain it to me.

"It's Irish history Rose. We can't deny it. It's who we are in the world. It doesn't mean we don't want to live in peace, but it has to be peace with dignity."

It gave me a lot to think about, not only on that evening but for many months to come.

[Note: this point - seminal for me to understand the mood at the time.]

Rose: The bar quietened down, and Wee Patrick introduced the band. After playing the reel, *The Morning Thrush* to get the crowd stamping, your dad announced they had a special guest with the family who was visiting from Scotland along with his cousin Siobhan. Siobhan waved to the crowd, and I sat blushing as he went on.

"I apologise because I only know a bit of one Scottish song and it's by Robert Burns. I'll sing what I can remember in

98

honour of our guest, and by great good
fortune, her name happens to be Rose."
I've never been sure if it was a coin-
cidence and he really did only know one
Burn's song, but I've always given him
the benefit of the doubt.
Then without musical accompaniment, he
sang out for the crowd:
O my Love is like a red, red rose
That's newly sprung in June…

At the end there was silence that
lasted for a heartbeat before the
cheers began, and I, who'd been squirm-
ing, was slapped on the back by various
people sitting at the table. Siobhan
winked at me. I didn't manage to recover any poise for the rest of the
evening, and if I hadn't been already
smitten with him when we walked through
Neil's cell door, I certainly was from
the moment of the serenade. After all,
Connor and Burns in a ruinous partner-
ship. What chance did I have?

[Note: I made an effort not to show emotion or frustra-
tion that would interfere with the story-telling—we had
to get through the first love and young adventures terri-
tory.]

Connor: The evening carousing ended at Neil's house after the bar closed. The singing stretched into the wee hours of the morning. Your mum eventually fell asleep on the sofa in the living room, but Siobhan woke her up by shaking her arm. I was sitting beside her. I'd worked my way to that position as the evening progressed.

Rose: I got to my feet, a bit unsteadily and Siobhan saved me as I pitched forward.

She made an attempt at a joke, "Watch the gammy-leg Rose."

Siobhan was used to being able to kid around without the need to self-edit, but she told me later she wanted to kick herself as soon as the words were out of her mouth.

"At least we know it's not the drink," she'd added, only emphasising the awkwardness of the moment.

Imprinted on my memory was the moment when I looked back and Connor mouthed, "Goodnight."

Siobhan led the way to one of the three mattresses laid out on the dining room floor for the girls to sleep on.

Connor: The drive back to the farm was uneventful, and I offered to pick the pair up to go to my mam's for tea later.

I'd told them your grandmother would be glad to see me too. She'd been giving me hell and asking if I've forgotten where my home is since I'd moved into my flat.

Rose: I was slowly gathering information. So, I thought, he has his own place, a flat. I was getting the picture.

Connor: And it was obvious I had to make a move or risk losing her. So, I was sure to remind them about coming over for tea, but I only got hold of Wee Patrick on the phone, so I was worried what he'd say, or more to the point, how he'd say it. He was the man for making a fool of me if he got the chance.

Rose: We were out in the yard, taking photos of Aidan who was standing on a flat-bed trailer attached to a tractor when Wee Patrick came out to relay the message.

"He's on his way—be here in about twenty minutes, and his mam's going to give you tea."

Siobhan started fussing and she gathered herself together. "You take care up there Aidan. I don't want you getting back home maimed in some way."

I remember how Aidan had borrowed an old leather belt to keep his jeans somewhere above his hipbones, and how he struck a pose designed to show his burgeoning arm muscles. This made his sister laugh as she added, "I definitely think there's some sign of life there Aidan. Just don't go getting into any trouble."

[Note: I recalled the snap I'd seen, a boy looking pink from the sun, a trace of freckles—a family trait. He looked so young and so at home in the yard among the vehicles and messy barns. Not quite a kid but definitely not a man.]

Rose: I chose for the occasion my best pair of slacks and a gypsy-style top.
Connor: It showed a little cleavage.

[Note: I detected a blush on Mum's face, but I was happy about the honest account they were giving me. Even if I'd heard most of it before, each was intentionally getting on board the courtship train.]

Rose: Siobhan, obviously appreciating the way the wind was blowing, came up beside me as I stared in the hallway mirror. "You're beautiful enough Rose, give the man a chance. We want him fit to drive."

And she went on making a joke of it, "I'll ride in the back seat if you promise not to dive on poor Connor while he's driving."

When I arrived downstairs, your dad was chatting to Aidan, advising him on how to keep from swallowing too much hay dust when he was following the bailer. "I always used a wet kerchief over my mouth. Old Paddy'll have one or two, I'm sure. Knock on his bedroom door, he'll be glad to see you."

Aidan had come back at him, "It'll make me look like one of the boyos that hang around in the Bogside," protested Aidan.

"The boyos aren't here to see you and no one's going to tell them. Better than getting choked in this heat and then as Rose and Siobhan appeared."

He said, "Well look at this Aidan, I'm getting to leave you here sweating to take out these fine-looking ladies. Be glad you're getting to work on those muscles though. You'll put those pasty Derry boys to shame when you go back." And with those words, he held the car door open while Siobhan climbed in the back.

Rose: I noticed your dad hadn't over-dressed. His hair was damp from being freshly washed. I could smell a musky aftershave which, fortunately given the heat inside the car, he'd applied sparingly. We wound down the windows to move around the languid air and headed along the narrow road into the town of Newry. I watched out of the window. We passed the Catholic Cathedral and went downhill to a row of small houses with brightly coloured doors and came to a stop at the one painted the colour of English Mustard. Dad kept up a running commentary, pointing out the location of his flat over an all-purpose convenience store, St. Joseph's High School where he taught, and the parish school he'd attended as a child.

Connor: She asked me if it was weird teaching at the school I went to as a kid, and I said the job and coming home to Newry had been handy, but I didn't think it would be for ever.

[Note: The word prescient flitted through my mind. It could not be avoided, and it sent a slight tremor over my neck and head. No one could have known then how history would take a hand.]

Connor: I said I thought it was best to stay close to Mam and Maxine because we had lost Da when I'd been in college; how he had been the rock in the family—working all his days as a carpenter, making sure they got a good education, taught me and Maxine to play the fiddle.
Rose: I hadn't been able to stop myself from asking what had happened, praying I wasn't going to hear a tale of some type of terrorist killing. And I also worried I had overstepped a boundary.
Connor: I wasn't the least annoyed, or hesitant. I told her he'd been hit by a drunk driver out on the street when he was unloading his van for the night.
Rose: I recall my words, "God, how terrible. I'm sorry for all of you. I don't know what we would do if something happened to my dad."

Connor: It would have been at this point that we piled into the house, and I introduced Rose to my mam. She explained Maxine had gone to Belfast for the day to shop. We got down to the usual tea, gossip, and the sharing of photographs. I was desperate to keep the conversation flowing so I told them the comical stories of why there was a patch in the living room ceiling and the time when I'd painted my bedroom walls purple. Mam added the story of how the kitchen had needed repainting after I'd tried to make her pancakes on Mother's Day when I was ten years old. Mam then produced a meal that made the kitchen table groan.

Rose: You should know, I was used to our own Scottish version of hospitality and so I wasn't easy to charm.

Connor: But it worked, didn't it?

[Note: Dad leaned over to touch Mum's arm, and she kissed his hand.]

Rose: And while everyone sat and had an after-dinner drink, Siobhan had flipped open the latest of the family' photo albums that sat on the coffee table. She asked if she could take home a recent picture of Connor and Maxine.

Rose: Later, back at the family farm, she slipped the prize into my hand, saying "Don't thank me. The drinks are on you when we meet again on the other side of the water."

Connor: At the end of the visit, I kissed the top of my mother's head and she waved from the door as we pulled away.

On the drive back, I drew up my courage to make a suggestion. I'm sure at the time, it would have seemed to come from nowhere.

"Would you two fancy going over to Amsterdam with me before the schools go back? I'd like to get a bit of time away and what with the band I can only spare about four or five days. Would the two of you be able to manage it? The hotels and eating out over there's cheap and I'll pay for the petrol and fares on the ferry."

Rose: Never mind surprise, I could hardly manage my excitement and I said, right away,

"A brilliant idea. I'll save a bit over the next few weeks, and Siobhan, it'd be great for you to get a break before you settle down in Glasgow. Say yes."

Connor: Outside the farmhouse we chatted about the logistics of the trip. I said I would take my car, meet Siobhan at the ferry and pick up Rose in Dumfries, and then we would head east to catch the ferry to Holland."

Then the next big thing happened—we exchanged phone numbers and promised to keep in touch so plans could be firmed up.

Rose: I made sure to add, "You'll be welcome to stay for a night with my family on the journey. Hopefully my mum will repay your hospitality with one of her famous steak pies."

As he drove away, I stared after the car long after Siobhan went into the farmhouse. She was waiting inside with Aidan and Wee Patrick when I entered the kitchen. The clan had broad grins splitting their faces.

Wee Patrick broke the silence, "He's broken a few hearts, Rose. He keeps himself fairly free of obligations. I like to think the band is his one true love."

"You three!" I said and something to the effect he was a perfectly nice guy and not to read anything more into it. Siobhan countered with, "You mean apart from the sudden invite for fun in the sin city of Amsterdam. Come to think of it, it's the first time he's ever

invited me anywhere. You realise, if I don't find a handsome Dutchman over there, I'm going to be the biggest gooseberry between you two."
I then begged. "Please tell me you'll go. I need to tell my family I'm going with you and your cousin. Can you picture me saying I'm going to Amsterdam with a guy I've only just met?
Siobhan slipped her arm around my shoulders, "It's a good job I really fancy the trip, so you're safe. Now let's get to bed so we'll be fit for the trip home tomorrow."

[Note: Mum shivered and paused to ask if I was cold because I was looking a bit pale. I told her I was okay and not to fuss. Dad flashed a look, no doubt I was sounding a bit too abrupt for his taste. To keep the peace, I got up to close the window anyway.]

Rose: Aidan spent two more weeks at the farm after we left. Siobhan and I went as far as Belfast together and then separated, Siobhan to Derry and me to Larne and the ferry home. Wee Patrick had taken us to the station in the multi-purpose van: shuttle bus for guests, band touring bus and occasional farm transport.

He had patted it lovingly. "There, the old girl's got you here in plenty of time." He added, "Rose, don't be a stranger, you'll be welcome back any time." They briefly hugged before he swung his cousin around.

I remember his final words. "Now don't you worry about Aidan. I'll take him up to Belfast myself and Brendan's going to meet us there. He'll be sound and we mean to get a bit more work out of the young fella before we send him back to your mother."

As he waved from the van's open window he shouted, "Send my best to Aunt Mary and tell her I'll visit Derry some time before Christmas."

"I will," Siobhan yelled as he rounded a corner, out of sight. She had a tear in her eye as she looked at me. "They're idiots but they're family and I love them."

I said, "I never did see, Old Paddy. Did you maybe invent him? That flu went on a while."

"I suspect he got to like laying up in bed and having whiskey brought to him at regular intervals. I don't grudge him the rest. It's been a hard-scrabble life farming on such a small scale, but he managed to raise a family there and to keep the place out of the hands of the banks. His boys don't mind indulging him a bit. They'd probably like it if their Mammy would take it easy, but I don't see it happening any time soon. The good thing is as long as they're alive I get to visit once a year, been doing it ever since I can remember. I have my doubts about whether Wee Patrick or Fergal will keep it on as a going concern. It'll be a sad day for me when it's gone."

I shuddered. "I don't even want to think about our farm passing out of the family. Lucky for me Young Walter's ready to step into our father's shoes. I forgot to say, he's getting married to a woman called Geraldine and the talk is he'll renovate one of the old dairy-mans' cottages and move in there when he marries. I hear the wedding's planned for next Spring. That'll be the first of my brothers and not before time. Walter's already 29, I didn't think anyone was going to land him.

Siobhan said wistfully, "We'd better get a move on in the romance department, or we'll be old maids before you know it." She made a mock gesture with an imaginary pen, "I'll pencil-in you and Connor for this time next year."

For safe keeping, I'd tucked the photo of Connor and Maxine into the pages of a book I was reading, and thoughts of Connor unsettled me for the entire journey. All the way through high school and university, I'd wondered about meeting the right man and how it would feel when it happened. Every time I felt interested in someone, I would ask myself, is this what love's like? Is this what people call love? In truth, all I knew about romance was from films, and the people in those stories seemed to know for certain when love arrived. But with the arrival of Connor I felt I'd been wise to wait for the feeling, that when it arrived, could not be ignored.

Connor: It is worth noting though, romance aside, the happily ever after didn't lie within easy reach.

Rose [laughing]: I knew little or nothing about the man and what I did know worried me. He was so… Irish. But the minute I pulled out the snapshot from inside of my book that day on the ferry, I knew this was different.

I expect it will be the same for you, A.J., when your time comes.

That evening, Henry was waiting for me in the car park and as usual, he rushed

over to help with my rucksack. We ban-
tered in the car, and I apologised because I hadn't managed to find any
gifts I liked for the family. Seizing
my moment, I added, "But don't worry
I'll have a better chance to shop when
I go away next."

"Oh?" said Henry.

"I'm going over to Amsterdam in August
with Siobhan and her cousin."

"My, you really are stretching your
wings. Two countries in as many
months."

"Yes," said I.

"Well, I expect you three girls'll take
care of each other." I allowed my big
brother the momentary comfort of his
error.

END OF NOTES

6. Sin City

Source: Transcript of conversation with Rose
Time Reference: 1970

After lunch, I prepared for the next phase of the narrative. Mum had just left Ireland and Dad behind. I'm sure she would have used the weekend at home to catch up on sleep, family news and laundry, and staying close to home, glad for the tranquillity broken only by music trickling its way from her young brother Thomas' room.

Mum and I were alone. Dad had returned to his study. I could hear him strumming on his guitar. Mum relaxed and took up the story while at the sink, me recording as she talked, she washing the dishes while I dried. The recording quality suffered as a result, but the physical activity kept the tension that stillness brings to a minimum. We had more background to expose, and I hoped it would become evident when things with Siobhan may have changed.

TRANSCRIPT POST- LUNCH CONVERSATION - ROSE

Young Walter and his fiancé Geraldine came for Sunday dinner the weekend after the trip to Ireland. This was the first time I'd met her, and knowing your Uncle Walter and Aunt Geraldine, I wondered how two such mild-mannered people had managed to send any kind of signal to each other, far less, one powerful enough to spark romance. Yet, there they were sitting in front of me, an engaged couple.

Right after dinner I saddled Prince and arranged to meet them at the cottage they'd begun to renovate. Actually, there were two semi-derelict cottages side by side to be knocked into one larger home. The walls were thick, the slate floors uneven, the plaster cracked, and the doors, if they opened at all, didn't close properly. I could see this was going to be an expensive undertaking. But mostly, I had a good feeling the family was going through a natural turn of the evolutionary wheel and accommodating the next phase in our lives.

"Don't worry Sis," Young Walter said, "I can teach you how to use a paint brush. I'm expecting repayment for all the times I drove you around when you were younger."

I was glad the expense of my education was over, and I still wonder if Young Walter had waited for me to graduate. It would be like him to be cool and strategic. I was used to seeing him poring over graphs showing milk yields and reports from our masters in all things milk production and sales, the Scottish Milk Marketing Board. Getting the timing right was his style.

That night, when I got back to the house, Thomas was outside yelling and miming the family code for, 'You're wanted on the phone.'

I thought it was likely to be Siobhan, or Mrs. McWhirter checking I'd be in the next day but was caught on the wrong foot when I heard, "Hi, are you there? It's Connor—Connor from Newry."

"Did you think I wouldn't remember you after two whole days?" I said, barely able to contain the relief he'd been the first to call. I'd initially made up my mind to wait for him to make the next move but to be honest, my determination had been waning.

Now, we weren't going to win any prizes for being great conversationalists. This is roughly how it went, and I can still remember my stomach being full of butterflies.

Connor came back at me, "Well you never know, do you? I'm really phoning to check you arrived home safely."

And I said something like, "I'm well. How about you?"

"Much the same really."

"Good."

Pregnant silence, and then I thought of something I could say. "I really enjoyed myself over there, and there's something I want to tell you."

I was jumpy and went from sitting on the bottom stair to leaning on the wall with my back to the kitchen where the family lurked.

"What? Please don't say you've changed your mind about Amsterdam."

"No, never, I'm looking forward to it. I wanted to let you know I got hold of the photo of you and Maxine from Siobhan. I hope you don't mind. It's a

lovely reminder and it's sitting on my
bedside table."
"Not at all, I'm flattered to be sitting there. I've that picture of you
with Siobhan, but I wouldn't mind another of you by yourself if you would-
n't mind sending me one."
"Let me take down your address."
That's about as much of the conversation as I remember, but I recall that
the next minute was ugly, spilling contents of the desk drawer onto the
floor, as I looked for a pen and paper,
and got the details from him.
 I was running out of anything sensible
to say, and what came out was something
pathetic like, "Thanks for phoning, I'm
looking forward to August."
God the relief when he came out with,
"Would it be okay if I phoned next Sunday? The band'll be back from a three-
dayer in Dublin, and I can tell you how
it went."
Of course, I agreed like a shot.
"I'll speak to you next week then. Take
care of yourself."
I put the phone down and bent double in
a controlled whoop of joy. When I got
to the kitchen, four pairs of eyes were
looking over their teacups. It seemed

like as good a time as any to get the
story out into the open.
"It was Siobhan's cousin, Connor."

*[Note: Mum sat down and leaned forward, which pres-
aged a change of attitude on her part. I could see her
eyes narrow as she went on, reflecting determination
nothing was going to spoil her enjoyment as she told this
part of the story.]*

"Oh," said your grandparents and Uncle
Henry all together—'Oh' as in, 'let's
see what she's got to say'.
"The one going with you over to Amsterdam?" Henry said, smiling, looking the
way torturers do when they play with
their victims.
I drew myself together.
"Yes, and before you ask, he's a
teacher in Newry and he's in the family
folk band."
I looked at Henry. I got the impression
my torturer was saying to himself--
"They always break eventually," but he
stayed silent.
"What's the name of the band?" asked
Thomas—God bless him.
Then I realised I'd never heard their
name. People had only referred to them
as The Family in my hearing.

"You know," I said. "I don't have a clue. I'll ask him when he phones next Sunday." And I poured myself tea and took it to living room to see if there was a film I fancied on the telly.

At least round one was over.

I'm sure I kept everyone in a state of high dudgeon as the date in August approached. I got the plans for the sleeping arrangements for the stop-over at my house worked out—Siobhan would sleep in my room and Connor would take the bottom bunk in Thomas'. I packed and repacked several times as I fussed about the likely weather in Amsterdam. I bought new jeans and shoes for the trip and I talked-up Connor's talents with the family and how a teacher was a terribly respectable job. I made a point of staring at Henry when I said this.

In the meantime, I spoke to Connor every week and was questioned each time. Henry was on full alert. He knew no one had ruffled my feathers this way before, and so this Connor was worthy of some brotherly attention.

And eventually, the cousins arrived together in Dumfries on the appointed day. I had pleaded with Henry to take me to the agreed rendezvous spot. The plan was for him to guide Connor back to the farm.

I saw Connor's Peugeot waiting in the car park and opened the car door before Henry had come to a full stop. The two men, Celtic to the core, hung back as Siobhan and I hugged and inspected each other's outfits. Then the men in turn, stiffly shook hands and introduced themselves. I stepped forward and kissed Connor shyly on the cheek. He returned the gesture and took my hand as we walked to the car. Siobhan diplomatically said she wanted to chat to Henry and Rose volunteered to travel in Connor's car. Henry tried to be friendly, but the brows drawn down gave him away.

Me? I was so happy.

[Note: Mum said, "I hope this isn't too much detail for you A.J—did you mean to get all this guff?"
I nodded.
"You did, Oh good."
But to be honest, I was glad to get out of the weeds]

So, getting back to the farmhouse, I could feel your gran and grandpa's eyes on us. Watching how we were with each other.

Your gran told me privately she was able to understand Connor's allure—with his dark eyes set in a boyish face, but she also said uppermost in her mind was, if we made a go of the relationship, would I move to Ireland and choose to convert to Catholicism. Of course, she didn't mention any of this on the day. I got that speech after we got back from Amsterdam.

I watched everyone very carefully over dinner, looking for every nuance.

Walter said, from the head of the table at dinner, "I believe we've both of you to thank for the hospitality you gave to our Rose when she was over there. We've never heard the end of how much she enjoyed herself."

Connor replied, "It was a great pleasure and Rose promised us your great pie, Mrs...."

"Please call me Peggy. I'm glad you enjoyed it."

"…I think it was the best chicken pie I've ever tasted. Was it from your own chickens?"

"It was," Peggy answered self-consciously. She caught his grin.

What a charmer, I thought.

I recall your uncle Thomas, was restless at the end of the table and managed to but in. "Connor, did I see a guitar in your car?"

"You did. Do you play?"

"No, but would you play us something?"

"I expect your family need some peace and quiet," said your dad, his neck getting red.

Your grandmother insisted. "We never get any musicians here. None of us have any musical leanings. Well, except for Rose who was in our church choir."

If she was testing for a reaction from Connor about my former church affiliation, none was forthcoming. They did not realise, like Siobhan, he was a nominal Catholic who would not flinch at a marriage across the religious divide.

I seem to remember we drifted through to the living room and Connor retrieved the guitar from his car. He taught Thomas how to play three chords.

"There," he said. "Your first guitar lesson. I wish I'd known you were interested. I've an old one at home I could have brought for you."

Thomas beamed.

Connor said, "Will I play you something?"

"Do you know anything by the Stones?" asked my brother.

"Not really. I'm famous for learning about four lines of a song and not being able to remember the words what come next. But I know, 'We All Live in a Yellow Submarine.' I learned it back when I was a student doing a school placement. Maybe I could teach you to play it someday." Connor began to play the Beatles Song and then played the Londonderry Air. It was sweet, so unlike the image of Derry I had witnessed.

Everyone listened quietly and politely applauded at the end. It was not quite the raucous atmosphere of the Newry farm, but this was my tribe. If it were possible for me to feel any happier at the scene in the family kitchen, I don't know how. I remember my dad wiping away a tear and deflecting attention by cleaning out his pipe. Your grandad is ever a sucker for a sentimental tune.

When the clock in the hallway struck 8:00, Henry suggested we go to the Burns Inn for a drink and over the next hour, he stopped only just short of a full-on interrogation with a bright light in your dad's eyes. He found out about his job security, his relationship with his widowed mother, how long he'd rented his own flat, whether his grandparents were still alive, and how often Connor visited the Republic. He also managed to wheedle out how Connor seldom attended Mass and then only to please his mam. Siobhan interrupted often enough to break the tension and when Henry left to use the toilet I begged for forgiveness.

"Don't worry Rose. I'm much rougher on Maxine's boyfriends."

And again, the silent internal whoop of joy. Did he really allude to himself as my boyfriend?

Connor pinked-up and said, "Yes, I did imply I'm your boyfriend. Cheeky, I'm sorry."

"No, it's fine. Good to know," and I covered his hand on the table with my own.

Henry was stopped on his way back to the table by a stylish young woman with red hair and false eyelashes. They talked for a while before he rejoined the group. There was silence on his return while the two women pointedly waited for some information.

Henry coughed, "That was Faye McConnell, she teaches biology at the same school as me."

Siobhan offered her un asked for words of wisdom, "You do realise she has the hots for you, don't you? You need to make a move Henry before she bats those fabulous eyelashes and tries to teach another guy about biology." She affectionately elbowed him in the ribs.

Henry muttered something no one could quite catch and changed the subject to his job teaching Maths and Physics at the high school in Castle Douglas. However, I noticed he glanced over at Faye as he finished his drink and made a point at waving as the four left the bar for home.

Siobhan winked at Rose and gave her the thumbs up sign before leaning in, "Only me left. Please God, make a rich Dutch guy sweep me off my feet."

I was relieved she wasn't jealous of Faye. She obviously had no designs on Henry.

[Note: It probably showed I was thinking—at last a glimpse of what is going on for Siobhan—and I asked Mum a direct question, relieved to be on track, as I saw it. "Did she seem happy to you now she had her degree and the promise of work in her chosen field?"]

Rose: I would say she was as happy as I had ever seen her. She was genuinely relaxed and seemed to like joking at Henry's expense. But with no malice, you understand. Check with your father if you like, but Siobhan and I were close, we were young, and we were happy.

And to get back to the story, a pre-dawn start for the east coast made sure we could board the early ferry to the Hoek van Holland and arrive in Amsterdam as night fell. Regardless of travel-weariness, we strolled after checking into the Hotel Roode Leeuw—along Damrak to the City's central rail station, stopping for *frites* with mayonnaise and Dutch beer. Tired, we still promised each other an early breakfast and a day of visiting the Van Gough and Rijksmuseum.

Siobhan scrunched her eyebrows at me as Connor went up to his room leaving us to take the elevator to our twin-beds. "What?" I snapped at Siobhan as I caught the look.

She asked me how many chances was I going to get to jump his bones.

[Note: Mum looked at me, adding an editorial detail: "You wanted to know how things were with Siobhan in this story, so be aware. I'm telling it to you without much revision. As I don't see your ears going red the way they

do when you're embarrassed, I'm assuming this isn't too uncomfortable for you. I'll go on." She sat and folded her arms looking ahead.]

I said to Siobhan, "Let's keep things in proportion, shall we. What we have is a long-distance relationship going here, and I don't want desperation to drive the pace."

The next day we took in as much walking and Dutch art as we could stand in one day. We agreed the next would be spent wandering alongside and cruising on the canals, and maybe taking a quick evening stroll through the red-light district. We agreed there was no point in visiting Amsterdam unless you took on board the whole tourist experience. Day three, we decided, would be devoted to gift buying, visiting Anne Frank's House, finding one of the famous flower markets and ending the evening in Dam Square for dinner. With plans agreed, Siobhan begged to be allowed to get into the bath first so she could soak her aching feet. Connor and I bid her goodnight and he snuck onto the bench beside me and placed an arm around my shoulders.

He said, "I noticed you limping again. It seems to come on at night."

"It's a permanent legacy of childhood polio. I was lucky it was only a mild dose, and it was caught early. The limp only comes on when my leg muscles are tired. And before you ask, I don't want to take it easy. I can handle a day or two of walking."

We chit-chatted about the day and even the silences were comfortable. I leaned against his arm but was fully awake when he said, "Rose, how do you see this going for us?"

I'd decided at some point to make no assumptions and to be glad to feel this happy. At the very least, I wanted to keep myself in check until I had a better sense of his feelings, but now he'd opened the bidding. It was my move.

"I honestly don't know, Connor. We hardly know each other, and I haven't dared think about it. So, if you want this to be a summer fling then tell me. It'll be fine. I realise the Irish Sea's a bit of a barrier to a serious relationship."

He said, "I don't feel like it's a summer fling. Do you?"

"No, but like I said, we could decide right now to think of it that way and move along."

He had taken the initiative. I must have given him enough encouragement for him to go on, "I've another suggestion and you need to forgive me because I'm a really practical person: what if we decide it's not just a summer thing, get back to our jobs and agree to see each other three times between now and Christmas. The plan shouldn't break the bank if we keep our budgets under control."

I sat up, fully alert and we talked about the practicalities—minimising the costs, etcetera. We agreed at Christmas we could make up our minds about the future.

Tired as I was, I struggled to prevent myself from taking a leap out of my seat. Instead, I said something like, "I'm all for taking it easy and getting to know each other a bit better. Here's to Christmas."

And facing each other, we drank down the last of our beers. "Now if it's okay, I'm going up for a bath and I'll see you later."

I'd made up my mind, on the spot, as your dad had been the one to put his cards on the table, it was up to me to take the next step. I won't elaborate on the details of the night for your benefit, but Siobhan gave me a thumbs up at breakfast when your dad and me walked in together.

On our last evening, sitting in Dam Square we looked at the front of the Royal Palace trying not to recall the pictures we'd seen earlier in the Anne Frank Museum, of people lynched there during the Nazi occupation. Siobhan and I had pinned small sunflowers from the market in our hair and as we strolled, Connor had his arms draped over our shoulders.

I truly believe Siobhan was beyond happy to be present at the birth of our relationship. I felt nothing but warmth coming off her.

Back at the hotel and never being a diplomat, she said, "Go, cement Celtic relations for all time."

When we parted in Dumfries, Siobhan stayed an extra night at the farm as she was going to get a train to Glasgow the next day to check out her flat and to find her workspace in Strathclyde. She wanted to be prepared for September. I watched Connor drive away along the track to the main road. I missed him before he turned on the road to the coast.

[Note: we took a comfort break and I rolled my neck. I'd stayed as still as possible, not wanting to miss a change of expression. I was glad to move around and I put away some of the dishes I'd dried and opened that window again. I checked my watch. This had been a long session but I suspect Mum was more pleased about how it was going than me. We sat down again to get back at the story we had paused.]

According to the plan, we met in Stranraer twice and in Newry once. Weekly phone calls became twice a week, and they were eventually supplemented by others when neither of us could wait to share a thought or plan.

Over the autumn months, your dad became the favourite teacher of the third-year girls, and I parlayed my volunteer position at the museum to assistant curator. Connor played with the family band, mostly over the border. Thomas and I rode out together on the ponies on the weekends I spent at home. I also kept my promise to help Young Walter and Geraldine, carting out rubbish from the demolitions and offering encouragement to Geraldine about colour schemes and kitchen appliances—all the time imagining the day your dad and I would be getting a house together.

Henry and your grandfather taught me to drive. I could tell Peggy was fretting about losing her girl to the man from the other side of the water. She knew me well, and in the way of many worried mothers, crossed her fingers and left the matter at that.

Connor spent the start of the school Christmas break at the farm with the family and then we travelled together to Ireland in the dwindling days of December to spend the remainder of the holiday there. Sleeping in his flat and partying with the family at the farm and elsewhere.

On January 2nd, I tore myself away and boarded the train on the first leg of the journey home. The long-distance relationship had been cemented by declarations of love during the stay.

"Don't worry, everything else is mere logistics," Connor reassured me. "The next steps will unfold. Let's just get to the summer."

The next phase involved monthly interludes at one or other port and an Easter break in Dublin with the band. Connor decided he should economise by moving in with his mother and sister and he informed his bandmates he would continue to take off one weekend a month and would be away for most of his summer vacation. I set about passing my driving test so I could move around independently.

The plan, mostly discussed on the phone, was to make the vacation time count. I could get only two weeks off, and I tagged them onto a long weekend which meant we could get away together for a decent stretch. The high point was those two whole weeks we would spend in southern France. There, the weather was kind enough to allow us to spend the nights under canvass.

In June, before we left, Connor spent time at the farm, and he felt like he paid for his keep by working with Young Walter on the cottage renovations. The roof was made sound and the interior walls were taken back to the stone. He got more tanned and ended each day caked in dust.

Keeping his promise to Thomas, he brought his old guitar and regularly tutored him. In a matter of a few weeks, we all got used to having him around. And when he was not there, we had Thomas' strumming as a reminder.

During that time in Dumfries, I introduced him to my man Robert Burns. On Sundays we toured around the sites in his car. We went to Ellisland Farm, where Burn's family had worked, and the Museum's Burns exhibition. We took picnics among the hills the poet knew so well. He learned the whole of *My Love is Like a Red, Red Rose*, guitar chords and all.

I think he may have gone back to Newry once to keep a band commitment. In fact, I know he did because Siobhan got the train down from Glasgow to get the ferry with him. She was going to visit her mother. She was staying in Glasgow for the summer to work, as I recall. It was maybe the third time she'd called in since she started work the previous September.

[Note: Long pause here – mum looked like she was doing mental arithmetic. I didn't disturb her, wanting her memory to flow without interruption. Without a question from me, she had volunteered an important detail.]

There was nothing exciting about her visits.
Before we left for France, Connor finagled a 'moment' with Henry by inviting him for a pint at the Burns Inn. I held back to allow the conversation without me hovering. Your dad had made friends as he worked side by side with

Young Walter, and now he wanted things with Henry to thaw a bit. I think Henry understood I was at a point in the relationship where my heart could be broken. So, he was still in protection mode and took the chance to get to the bottom of Connor's intentions. The two young lions in my life squared up across a table in the pub.

Connor told me he was the first to put his cards on the table.

He said he'd spilled out something to the effect, "Henry, I know we've been dancing around the subject with each other, but I want you to know for sure, I love Rose. This is it for me. My da, God rest his soul, was a man I looked up to. It's too bad you won't get to meet him, but he was a great family man. He took good care of my sister and me. He bought my mother a box of chocolates every Friday night. That's the stuff I'm made of. I'm in this for the long haul.

And before you ask, we don't know where we're going to live. We gave ourselves 'til this summer so we could be sure of each other. I *am* sure Henry, and by the end of the summer I'll know if Rose is too. The other thing I need to clear up is about religion. Neither Rose nor I are church-goers, and I know it's hard when you hear about the mess in Ireland, but I'm no part of that. Sure, I want my country to get to a place of peace and dignity, and although I am sometimes tested, I don't support the shedding of blood." Your dad was probably a lot more polished than I'm making him out to be.

And Henry's only question. "Why pick Rose?"

As far as I understand it, he got a straight reply "I love many things about her, including the level head she has on her shoulders, and I realise it comes from the family she was brought up in. Can I ask you to trust us? We'll make the right decision about where we marry when the time comes. We don't care about religion enough for it to cause a rift between us. We're happy to have found each other and we'll dance together at any family wedding, any church, any time. I promise you won't lose Rose because of me."

He said it was hard to read Henry's face, and went on, "And when the time comes, I'll talk to your father. That will be when Rose wants me to. For now, I hope we can shake on it."

I imagined him stretching out his hand and Henry taking it firmly.

Things must have gone quite well because on the drive home, Henry told Connor he hoped he'd make it over for Young Walter's wedding in October and said he needed help to plan a stag-night.

"Walter's not a guy to let his hair down. We'll need to be sneaky."

At that time, the talk between me and your dad was about getting engaged at Christmas. We didn't discuss the length of the engagement nor the wedding itself, but when we got back from France, we spoke to Walter and Peggy and assured the family we would do some hard thinking about our plans before Christmas.

It was a lovely moment. Peggy hugged your dad, and she sniffled a bit. Connor comforted her and promised she wouldn't be losing me, and it was more likely she would get sick of the sight of him. Walter put down his pipe and rubbed his hand down the side of his trousers. My two men shook hands and he said to both of us we would need to let him know when we needed his help and support, and he would always do his best for us.

"Don't worry Walter," said Connor. "We'll have time to plan the wedding. The main thing now is for me is to bring my mother over here for a visit. She's been giving me earache worrying about what will become of Rose and me."

Peggy answered, "I don't blame her. It's hard watching your kids go their own way. Why don't you bring her over to stay with us for Young Walter and Geraldine's wedding in October?

"We'll also get you and your mother to meet my parents. Rose is my dad's favourite, so he'll put you through your paces."

Connor joked with her to lighten the mood a bit. "I hope you'll be able to handle two Irish people under your roof."

In September, I visited Newry. Your dad had managed to keep the engagement under his hat until then as we wanted to speak to his mother together. Your grandma hugged me and wagged her finger.

"I knew you two were keeping something back from me."

But no matter how much she may have been worrying, she held herself in check, deciding the talk about the wedding ceremony, and in which church it

140

would be held could be postponed to another day. She knew Connor. My belief is she knew Connor was his father's son, and I mean by that, he would try to do the right thing for everyone. She also knew he would not be told what to do by her or any of the elders of the family.

However, she did not hold back the one thing she felt would help join me to her family and offered us her mother's sapphire ring. She said we should feel free to use only the stone if we would like a fresh setting and she looked so relieved when I said, without hesitation I might add, "Yes."

The sentiment of this gift overwhelmed me. After all, she had a daughter. It was of more meaning and value to me than shopping for something new on the high street. I was not Irish, and I was not a Catholic, but I learned over time she knew the moment I accepted her offer, I was the right woman for her son. Now, as I recall, Siobhan also got an invitation to Walter's wedding which she had to decline because of a European planning conference being held in Paris. I was sad because this was the first time since our days at university we would be apart for an important occasion in either of our lives. But I promised to send her pictures, and in the letter I said, "We're getting engaged."

Siobhan phoned the day she got the mail and almost burst my eardrum screaming, "When? When?" and she vowed to call in at the farm on her way to Derry to spend Christmas and the month of January with her family.

I remember us talking a bit about Aidan. She said, "I need to focus on him for a while. He's left high school now and I want him to think about getting a college place in Glasgow." She told me things were bad in the Bogside, especially since the Brits had started interning terrorist suspects.

She wanted him and Mary out of there but thought she would stand a better chance getting him to move. Apparently, her mother said she didn't want the thugs driving her out of her own country.

Siobhan had no difficulty in referring to 'the Brits' when speaking to me and it caused no tension between us. It was shorthand and meant nothing to me.

In truth though, this kind of update from Northern Ireland typically prompted a period of worry which I tried never to show to Connor. Nevertheless, I was anxious about Siobhan's family, all the Patricks, and the increased violent activity in Newry's border country. I was concerned about your dad travelling back and forth to the mainland, an activity that could attract the attention of the security forces who watched the sailings. They noted who made frequent trips and whether those trips tied into terrorist incidents.

[Note: I'd let her talk and now I felt I needed to ask a key question, the one which I wanted to speak volumes -- 'were you also worried that Siobhan was also going back and forth.?]

Of course, I was, but she didn't always tell me when she was travelling, so the worries I had for her were more general, vague. I'm sure I mentioned my worry to her. I'm sure I wouldn't have missed that. But I don't particularly remember where or when I said it and I do know Siobhan would have fobbed me off with a gesture or a laugh.

[Note: Mum hesitated for a while before shaking her head to bring herself back.]

And, as it happened Siobhan didn't manage to keep her promise to visit at

Christmas. She flew directly from Glasgow Airport to Derry and apologised for needing to work right up to Christmas Eve so she could take a long break at home with her mother in January. I was disappointed. I wanted her to share the celebration with us.

You'll remember me telling my ring was designed and made in Dumfries by the father of a boy I'd been at high school with. Two small diamonds on either side of the sapphire. Connor collected it on Christmas Eve. He didn't get down on one knee but gathered the whole family at the Christmas tree as he placed the ring on my finger. On Boxing-Day we left for Newry and a party at the farm with the whole gang except for the Derry contingent who, given the rising tensions in the country, felt it best not to leave the house unattended.

Siobhan missed both parties and I never got to see her face to face before the tragedy happened.

END OF RECORDING

[Faced with the escalating violence in Ireland, it was an abrupt end to a charming love story. We were introduced to a terrible looming sadness we would have to face. I had one question in my mind, and I asked her a final

question—for the moment. "Would you say she was cooling on the friendship at this point?

Mum answered, "Definitely not. She was very busy, that's all. We were back and forth on the phone a lot."]

7. Aidan

Source: Notes from conversation with Connor - father
Time Reference: 1972

We were losing daylight, my backside ached, and I asked Mum if she wanted to stop. She nodded. I noticed her limp as she went over to the sink to draw herself a glass of water. On cue, Dad came downstairs with a bundle of old newspapers to put in the re-cycling bin. The concentrated smell of newsprint and ink momen-tarily took me back to my days as a cub reporter, a job I combined with being a part- time blogger.

"Still going strong?" he asked.

"I was going to suggest you and I go for a pint and then get some curry to bring back. Save anyone cooking dinner. What d'you say Mum?"

"Fine with me. The only thing other that happened before 'Aidan...' was I came home, and we all went back to work—with me showing off my ring."

She held her hand out in front of her to admire it. I smiled, enjoying the pleasure she still got from its glint in the light. I was used to her snappy retelling of facts and realised it was time for a change.

"Maybe your dad would be best to fill you in at this point. He was in a better position than me to see what happened from all sides." What about it, Connor?

Dad went over to the back of her chair and massaged her neck. "I'll do that. It's definitely a story best taken with a modicum of alcohol."

The flow of the story telling was going my way. I really wanted to walk, to give my brain an extra boost of oxygen. We both had good outer wear and the rain had pulled back to what the locals called 'a slavery wind.' Within twenty minutes of striding out, we were brushing the fine mist off our jackets inside the door of the Burns Inn. I remember Dad saying with a sarcastic overtone, he was glad I'd decided not to dress up, doubtless referring to my well-worn jeans with holes below each knee. I fobbed him off with some joke about getting my wear out of my clothes made me an echo-warrior.

Laughing, we entered the lounge, situated there since time began. The same lounge Peggy and Robert, Rose's mum and her biological dad, had sat in all those years ago. I ducked my head to avoid the low lintel. We were alone. The little room had space for no more than three tables and a solitary picture of Burns. The man looked haughty, a bit more middle class than he could rightfully lay claim to. The wood panelling had been darkened by years of cigarette smoke and wood fires. Behind us, there was a heart, crudely carved with initials BA & L, whoever they were.

Dad went to the hatch in the wall to get access to Colin, the owner who was mostly focused on the adjacent public bar.

"No guitar tonight then?"

"Nah. I'm with my boy." He nodded in my direction.

Colin craned his neck around the gap to give me a nod. "The journalist?"

"That's right."

"I'll bring the drinks over."

Dad came back to the table, and I pointed at the portrait of Burns.

"I saw something on the TV a couple of weeks back. Apparently that portrait isn't a great likeness."

"How would they know?"

"Somebody made a cast of his skull all those years back when he was reburied in the mausoleum. And recently they gave it to an expert at Dundee University who does those forensic reconstructions. Apparently, he'd have looked a bit more thick-set, like a farmer. More Walter than the guy on the wall." I nodded at the portrait.

"So, he's been touched up?"

"Seems like it. I'm surprised Mum didn't say."

Collin came through the door, tossed two cardboard beer mats down on the table and put our pints on top. He went back through to the public bar and left us alone, with only the murmur of life from the bar next-door to provide some ambient noise, and with the fug of his cologne. I suspect he'd leaned a bit too heavy on the spray action. Dad winked at me in mute understanding.

I changed gear to steer us closer to the subject at hand. "I'm glad to get out of the house. I wanted us to be able to talk straight without derailing the issue by worrying about upsetting Mum."

"Not bothered about upsetting me then?"

I hadn't thought about that point but said without thinking, "Of course I am. He was your cousin after all, but for some reason, not so much. Is that fair?"

I stopped talking long enough to give him a chance to reply but he took a drink, and looked straight at me and said, "I've thought about Aidan a lot since you arrived, and if it is going to be written by anyone, I think I want his story written by someone who gives a damn. So, I'm feeling okay about telling you how I saw what happened—and in as much detail as I can remember."

He began to play with his beer mat, working it into the table with his fingers between sips.

"It's been a long time since I've thought about it in any details. Mum and I seem to have an unspoken agreement to skirt round it."

"I noticed that," I said.

Giving him the nod, I turned on the recorder for backup and focused my time in conversation, watching his reactions. I wanted to note how he was dealing with the questioning, not only to hear the words of the story. I was looking for any clues that might help me with a deeper understanding about his and Mum's relationship with Siobhan. But for Dad, it was obvious that this moment was purely about telling the story of the tragedy of Aidan's death, and to tell it in a way that honours the young man and his life.

NOTES FROM CONVERSATION WITH CONNOR – BURNS INN

AJ: I've got the whole bit about how you and Mum met and the long-distance courtship during the troubles, but I need to talk to you about that day. I don't think I've ever had the una-bridged version—and, by the way, that's totally understandable.

[Note: Dad, looking stern, didn't reply directly to the question.]

Connor: I need to check something. Would you reassure me about your re-spect for the dead and more to the point, for us still living when you write about us?

AJ: Fair question. I don't know if or how this will be published. In fact, I don't even have a clear picture of who the audience is. But I will promise you, nothing will go outside of the three of us unless you and Mum approve. And that could be tough for me to stick to because I might end up with a different view—or maybe interpretation of the facts—than you do.

[Note: I looked straight at him. I had put him on notice there could be difficult territory to be explored. He met my gaze. I blinked first.]

Connor: Care to give me a hint?

A.J: "Sure. I'm thinking about Siobhan—was her death connected to Aidan's? This leads me to ask was she keeping secrets? I have a feeling there must be a trail between the two deaths no one has perhaps dared to explore in the intervening time. At least no one who's spoken to me. Aidan's death was a travesty, but we know the ups and downs of it. But the mystery of how Siobhan died is different. It's unsolved, and the question that screams to me is, WHY? Why did she die and why is no one pressing for the answer?

While you guys are still around, I want us to have a frank talk about how much anyone knows and I want to have your opinion on record, even if, in the end, it's only for me.

I don't know how you feel, but I for one, don't want what you believe happened to Siobhan to get swept away because some bloody official report about how Aidan died has been written and put on the public record.

Don't get me wrong, I think that's a good thing, but it doesn't tell whole the story—of how bullets can carry on wounding long after they leave the gun. And it doesn't help me understand what happened to his sister. She, too, needs her portion of justice.

[Note: I paused to check how my statements were going down by looking in his eyes. He looked up for a second and then resumed playing with his beer mat. He screwed his eyes up, his face a mask of sadness. I could read nothing into his expression but grief.]

A.J: "Look at our family since the day Siobhan was killed. Mary's gone, Brendan's lost, you and Mum carry a sorrow I can almost feel at times. In my more fanciful moments, I even think Walter and Peggy worry what might happen to us if we were ever to find out everything there is to know. Peggy has a 'don't ask don't tell' look you cannot miss."

[Note: Here was the nub, I knew it. I could almost taste it. I let what I said hang in the air for a while. I know sometimes the art of an interview is knowing when to be silent. This was one of those times. I had made a statement about what I feel was at stake. Dad did not look up.

He fiddled with the beermat until I pushed forward in the chair and rolled up the sleeves of my sweater to show the tattoo of a serpent Mum wasn't too pleased about. Time to press my point. I leaned in.]

A.J: "And do you think those paratroopers who did the shooting on Bloody Sunday went back home and resumed their life. I'd put any money there's another lot of damaged lives limping about somewhere over here on the mainland, or who're giving orders to some other bunch of poor assholes who mostly want the regular employment the army gives."

[Note: he banged the edge of the beermat on the table. It's clear on the recording—thunk, thunk, thunk.]

Connor: And do you think you're going to solve their problems, too?
A.J: Hell no. But there again, you never know the ripple effect of telling the truth, and I'm prepared to leave that kind of analysis for the moment and focus on the story. You lived in Newry back then, and you surely have a bit of the story of the reverberations of the Troubles I want to capture. And believe me, it worries me it involves digging around in your personal life to get at some truths you maybe haven't

wanted to face. For instance, did someone betray someone else and is that somehow connected to how Siobhan died?

So, if you're ready, let's get to it. The day he died. Aidan. The one you named me after.

Connor: First, you need to get a picture in your mind of what it was like in Northern Ireland from the late sixties and on into the seventies. In case you've forgotten: people marching for civil rights, Catholics wanting a fair chance at the vote and at getting a decent job; Orangemen wanting to march through areas that poked provocatively at underlying danger, wanting a good scrap among the local yobs; and the Royal Ulster Constabulary not open to Catholics, seeming to do their best to make sure the civil rights folk got a good beating whenever they could. There's more than one video you can probably get online, of a march being directed by the RUC, forcing a march into a narrow lane where some yobos were waiting to beat the shit out of them. And young men on both sides starting riots in the streets that ended in bloodshed and sometimes death.

Then, as the Provos began to get more militant, the government banned all demonstrations. And at the start of 1972, Owen Cooper, the M.P. for Derry, a Protestant, who got some respect because he was prepared to stand up for civil rights across the board, organised a demonstration. He dashed about trying to make sure it didn't become a vehicle for the Provos or anyone else to use to start trouble.

That was the lead up to the day we're talking about.

Now, Rose and I hadn't planned to meet until Valentine's Day that year, and she wasn't expecting a call from me on the afternoon of Sunday January 31st. I was supposed to phone the next day for a chat. She would have known as soon as she got the call and from the tension in my voice something was wrong.

A.J.: So when you called her, was it because of what happened to Aidan?

Connor: Of course. I didn't want her to hear about what happened from the TV.

At the other end of the phone, I could hear the evening News was on the TV in her living room.

She said, "Hi, you're lucky to catch me. I've come in from giving the stables a good mucking out."

I knew then she'd been out of range of any news broadcasts, and I didn't know what to say.

She spoke up first. "Connor, is there something wrong?"

It took me a while to step over the chasm between us. The receiver felt like a lead weight in my hand, and even after the pause to gather myself, I could only summon austere, flat tones. "Aidan's been shot by the army. He died in hospital."

A.J.: What happened then?

Connor: Aiden Joseph, will you let me tell this my way.

[Note: I sat back and listened as I watched the tears well up in his eyes. The room was quiet. Thank goodness, no one came in to check if we wanted a beer order.]

Connor: I heard Peggy barrel into the hallway and while Rose was still holding the phone asked, "Is it the Rossville Flats where Siobhan's family lives?" Rose stayed silent and Peggy rushed on. "There's been a terrible riot and shots have been fired. They're saying a lot of people are dead."

Then Rose said to me, "Connor, where are you?"

"In Newry, and I doubt whether I'd be able to get into the Bogside even if I tried."

Rose must've been thinking fast. "I'm coming over tonight. Don't leave Newry it can't be safe."

That brought me to my senses. "No. No. Rose don't you come over here right now. Stay put and try to get in touch with Siobhan. I don't have her number in Glasgow. I'll phone back later tonight."

Then I couldn't hold it together any longer, and while Rose clung on to the phone, I bawled like an infant. I slid down until I was sitting on the hall carpet with my back against the wall.

"Connor, please stay with your mother and Maxine. I'll do my best to find Siobhan. Promise me you'll stay put until we've a better idea of what's going on. Please, promise me!"

I gathered myself together enough to say, "I'll be here. There's nothing anyone can do in Derry right now. I love you. Please try to reach Siobhan."

"I love you Connor, stay safe," And she replaced the receiver in its cradle.

Rose then had the job of telling her family Siobhan's brother Aidan, had been shot by the army outside of the flats and was dead. Seventeen, she said. Siobhan was trying to get him a place in a welding course at a college in Glasgow. She hoped he would come over in the Spring. Now he's dead.

[Note: *Dad paused here. I let the silence sit for a while.*]

A.J.: Do you know what Mum and her family were thinking when they got the news?

Connor: Rose and I talked about it afterwards. She told me how it went. Peggy had said, "Connor is a wonderful man, and I can tell you love each other, but I'm so scared about you going over there and especially settling after you're married. I couldn't stand the worry. Please God, don't go and live there, Rose. We'll let you move in here together or you can buy a place. We'll help until you get on your feet. Please tell me you won't go there to live."

No doubt Rose cried. She said she couldn't answer her mum. She was afraid there might not be an answer where it was possible for everyone to be happy. Rose rang Siobhan's flat in Glasgow with no answer, neither from Siobhan nor from either of her two flatmates.

As she put the phone down for the third
time in an hour, she realised Siobhan
might not even be in Glasgow. She'd
been planning to spend the whole of
January in Derry, doing some work
there.

Rose phoned me at home. I was mad with
the frustration of not being able to do
anything.

"Hello, did you reach her?"

"No," she said. "I've tried three times
but there's no answer. Are you sure
she's in Glasgow? She might have been
in Derry when it happened."

Now I hadn't thought of that. I said,
"I'll keep trying to get through to her
mother's place but its pandemonium.
Will you keep phoning her flat in Glasgow?"

Rose said, "Of course I will. Have you
heard anything else at all?"

I said, "No. We're listening for news
on the telly. All we see are roadblocks
and soldiers and a piece they keep
showing of a priest waving a white
hanky to bring an injured man out to
where there was an ambulance. You could
see it was an older man who was wounded
but I've no idea what it was about.
Anyway, I should get off the phone in
case someone is trying to get through.

Let's only ring this evening if either
of us hear from Siobhan."
But neither of us managed to connect
with her. As it happens, Siobhan had
heard the news while she was waiting at
the airport for a plane heading to
Glasgow. She'd turned around and somehow got back to the house through the
chaos. On Monday morning, before Rose
left for work, I phoned her to say
Brendan had phoned to say Siobhan was
with her mother, in the Bogside. Rose
asked me when the funeral was to be.
I said, "We're waiting to hear. There
needs to be an autopsy. This is going
to be a mess, Rose. There were thirteen
killed, more injured. Half of the dead
were seventeen years of age."
"Will you let me know the arrangements?"
I tried to get control of the situation
by saying, "Rose, my love. You cannot
come to Derry for the funeral. It's
like there's a bomb waiting to go off.
I don't particularly want my mother or
sister to be there either. We're argu-
ing that one out right now."
And then she blurted out, "God Connor,
I want you to come over here right
now."

I had to be calm. "It won't work Rose. I need to be with the family for the next while."

[Note: I noticed he'd started to shred the damp beermat and I got a brief historical foot note (typical Dad) while his hands worked frantically.]

For the next few nights, we watched the nightly news as the reporters dug backwards into what happened and the repercussions. Now we know the whole story, the march that had preceded the incident. As I said, it'd been a civil-rights demonstration against internment without trial. The organisers intended it to be a peaceful protest, in spite of the fact marches and demonstrations were banned by the government. Of course, the British soldiers said they had been fired at first, others that that was a lie. Ivan Cooper told a press-conference the government should know the actions of the soldiers had killed the civil rights movement in Northern Ireland, that things in the North of Ireland would inevitably shift, and in a chilling prophesy he added, they had given the IRA the greatest boost they could imagine.

A.J.: This is probably a stupid question, but what was the mood of the family, Mary, Brendan, Siobhan?
Connor: We were too deep in grief to be able to take part in whatever political debate there was. Anger came later, for me any way. Not even the death of my own father had struck the note the taking of Aidan did.

[Note: Long Pause – I waited as he took his time before picking up the thread of the story. Nothing in his silence invited comment or interjection.]

Connor: On the morning of Aidan's funeral, Rose flew into Derry Airport without me knowing and against her family's wishes. She took a taxi to the battle-scarred Rossville Flats. I think Maxine answered the door. I couldn't believe my eyes.
I muttered something like, "I told you not to come," but hugged her close.
"Where else would I be?" Rose said into my shoulder.
Siobhan didn't seem to register her friend's arrival and stayed by her mother's side.
A.J.: By that, do you mean she was overcome with grief or was it more like

she was staying stiff-backed and contained?

Connor: I think by that time it was mostly about containing herself.

A.J.: Did Mum say what it was like getting through to the Bogside that day?

Connor: I seem to remember her telling me there were more troops at the airport, on the tarmac, everywhere, and a checkpoint on the road into the city. The whole place seemed to me to be on lockdown but we were family of the deceased and so we probably got through the crowds without the hassle other people were put through. At some point, things got really tense when the word got round somebody had set fire to the British Embassy in Dublin.

Now let me go on while I have a clear picture in my head.

Rose sat with Maxine and my mam in St. Mary's Church, and I helped bear young Aidan's coffin on my shoulder away from the Funeral Mass for eleven of the victims. She stood with me at Aidan's grave and stayed for the wake at their parish church hall. It was like any funeral I've ever known. We all swapped tales of the boy with snake-hips who couldn't ever quite manage to keep his jeans from falling down. I thought my heart would break but I kept it together.

When people were doing the rounds of offering condolences, Siobhan seemed to be somewhere else. If I didn't know her better, I would have thought she was medicated. But I think she was using whatever strength she had to keep herself together for the sake of her mother. Mary was allowed to do the wailing for all of us.

Rose went over to speak to Siobhan, tried to hug her but was put off by her stiffness. It was like she couldn't accept kindness. Maybe she was afraid she'd breakdown and make a scene, or she didn't want to draw sympathy away from her mother. I couldn't truthfully say.

A.J.: What did you do?

Connor: I left her alone. I got the message from how she reacted to Rose, her best friend. At some point she disappeared. She'd probably had enough and, as I say, I let her be. To this day, I don't know whether that was the right thing to do.

At 6 o'clock, Rose kissed me goodbye and boarded a taxi for the airport. She got back to safety, to the farm, while only a short plane-hop away, our world in Ireland boiled over. More troops, more gunfire, more deaths.

A.J.: How were things between you two after that?

Connor: As we had planned, and after days of telephone conversations strained by sadness, Rose and I met for Valentine's Day in Stranraer. It was the first time we were able to talk at any length since the tragedy, now being called Bloody Sunday. We checked into our usual bed and breakfast. I was anxious Rose would want to find a way out of our engagement. After all, I don't think she ever imagined the violence would come so close.

My state of mind that evening had not been helped by the fact I'd been detained for questioning by the security men at Larne. It was an hour's ordeal I'd half expected. Everyone had been talking about the increase in the checks and the longer delays. Even with the extra time I'd allowed, I only just managed to get aboard the ferry in time for the sailing.

Rose asked me what they wanted to know. I said, "For sure, they know I go back and forth a lot and they wanted to know my business on the mainland. They're suspicious of people making short trips like I do. They searched my bag, and they wanted to know your family's name. I had to tell them. I hope's okay."

"'Course it is. We've nothing to hide. Let them ask us."

And for the first time ever I slid down the rabbit hole of despair. In the past, I'd been the one who told her and her family it would all work out. Now I was done.

"God, I'm so sick of this Rose." She stayed silent, thank God, because I needed to take things at my own pace.

"I'm about ready to give up. There's no choice for me now. The more I go back and forth, the more I'm going be stopped. It's only a matter of time before you get questioned every time you make the crossing. I've already told my mother I'm going to see the school year out and then get some work over here. I can't do it any more Rose. It's too fucked-up over there. Me staying in Ireland won't make a difference one way or the other, and I can't ask you to give up what you have here for the kind of life I can only see getting worse." She came around to my side of the bed held me close. Still, she said nothing, but a good nothing if you know what I mean.

"This is how I see it. I'll come over at Easter and get Henry's advice about finding a job. I'll take anything and I'll find a place to stay. I don't want to rush you into marrying me. I know it all sounds a bit desperate."

Then she spoke. I was relieved. "We'll do what we always do, Connor. We'll be pragmatic. You have family here now. You'll be welcome. I know my folks. We'll work it out."

She had some questions about Siobhan and my mother—how they were coping.

I found it easier to tell her about Mam. "She's still in shock about Aidan and keeps saying, 'I don't blame you son. I don't want another of us to die here.'"

I hadn't seen Siobhan since the funeral, and so I can't tell you anything about her state of mind.

A.J.: Did you worry?

Connor: Of course, but I felt shut out after the funeral. All I know is at some time she went back to her work in Glasgow. I don't know when exactly, but she eventually started calling Rose again. I didn't think much more about her.

The next morning, instead of staying in Stranraer, Rose drove us in the car she'd borrowed from Geraldine, to the family farm in Dumfries. Rose wanted us to spend the soggy February day tucked up in the warmth and security of her home. Everyone swarmed around us and I felt the healing might possibly start. On Sunday, Rose drove me to the ferry terminal well in advance of the time to catch the last sailing. She waited by the car until the ship sailed.

On the phone late that night, when everyone in both households were in bed, she told me how she watched the lights of the ship heading for Larne disappear, and had wondered how two places, separated by a narrow, wild ribbon of water, could be so different. On her shore, the peace of the countryside was undisturbed by bullets, bombs, and terror, whereas I had sailed back to a land where they were the unholy trifecta that passed for normality.

END OF NOTES

Dad looked at me. The beermat was in tatters. His faced was pitted with grief. I wanted it to be enough but knew there was more to find out about this time in Siobhan's life.

8. Newfoundland

Source: Conversation with Rose-mother and Connor-father
Time Reference: 1972

Dad and I picked up chicken korma, a lamb curry, rice, and naan bread, and we walked home. The night was typical for Dumfries at the time of year. Mist halos diffused the light from the streetlamps, and I wrapped my scarf around my neck and up to my chin.

Mum was standing at the window in the sitting room. The plates had been heated and the kitchen table set. She took the food bags from me as Dad and I divested ourselves of our damp coats and boots. The heat fogged up my glasses. She took them off my face, wiped them on her apron, and put them back on my nose.

"Are you leaving for Edinburgh tomorrow?" Dad asked.

"I think I'll get going right after lunch. I'll get back in time to do some work."

He made a welcome offer. "I'll take you to Lockerbie to get the train. You should look up the times before we retire for the night."

"That'd be great."

In the easy way families have, we took the lids off the food containers and started to dish up our own platefuls, weaving around each other.

As we sat down Mum caught my attention by moving her face into my sightline. I would have been glad to leave our next chat until breakfast, but I suspect she was anxious to hear how things stood after Dad's and my session on Aidan.

"So, did he give you everything you need?" she asked.

"Mostly, but I'd like to bring the story forward a bit—to talk about what happened with Siobhan after Aidan died. Was there still the close contact between you or did things change? And, of course, when did you last see her? Now, I can wait 'til the morning. You must have had your fill of it."

"I'd sooner get it over with and then tomorrow maybe you'd help me clear a couple of flower beds and turn over the compost." There was an edge to her voice which I took to be an indicator she was reaching the end of her tether. And didn't want to sleep on the retelling for another night We were heading for the point in the story when Siobhan's death would have to be faced. I said, "it's a deal."

172

Dad had a mouth full but gave me the thumbs up sign.

I licked the thumb I'd got mixed up with the sauce on my plate and found the voice memo feature on my phone this time. I'd started to worry about hitting capacity on the recorder.

TRANSCRIPT – CONVERSATION ROSE AND CONNOR

Rose: I find it hard to remember exactly how often Siobhan visited the farm that year. But then, we went on a trip to Newfoundland. Do you remember me mentioning that to you?

[Note: I nodded – I'd seen the photographs of two girls on a wild headland—hair blown back off their faces, dressed for both sun and wind. I took the chance to ask how the trip had come about.]

Rose: I'll get to that.
I understood how hard it must have been for her—the shock of losing her brother to a violent death. I knew she'd need time to recover, and I had been sending letters to keep her up to date with what was happening at my end. I patiently waited for her to get in touch when she was able to. I'll admit it made me feel sad a distance had opened up at a time when she was devastated, and I was happily planning my future. I'd feel a wave of guilt from time to

173

time but never thought there was anything weird about the silence at her end. Nor did I ascribe anything callous or uncaring to it. For my part, I felt nothing but sympathy and understanding.

Eventually, in your dad's and my mind, the initial pain of Aidan's death lessened as the Spring progressed. It became tucked into the backwaters of our minds.

As planned, he talked to Henry during the Easter break about his prospects of finding a local teaching job, and was encouraged to hear at the very least, he could expect to find steady work as a substitute teacher until a permanent post opened up.

Henry offered some straight advice. "My thinking, though, is to set a date for the wedding. The school boards will look on you with less suspicion if you're getting married to a local woman. Unfortunately, that kind of hesitancy on their part is how the troubles across the water might play out here."

The final plans for the immediate future were made over the dinner table, and before bed, they were finalised. He would come over in the summer and stay with Walter and Geraldine, who were living in their renovated cottage by that time, and we would then marry at Christmas.

The next morning, I remember Connor slinging his bag over his shoulder as he walked out to Henry's car.

He said, "Right, you two ladies, I'll leave you to plan a wedding. Tell me where and when to turn up, and I promise to be there."

I waved. My tears streamed as Henry drove him away to catch the ferry so that I would make it to work on time. My grief was for him, his family, and a longing for the time when we would be together.

Next came a pleasant surprise. That very afternoon Siobhan called me at work. I admit I held my breath hoping there was no more bad news.

The conversation went something like:

"Hi. It's me. I wanted to catch you before I head into a department meeting. I've had an unbelievable stroke of luck. I entered a contest to win a pair of plane tickets and a week in a hotel in Newfoundland. My mother won't leave Derry because she's asked the Council for a change of houses. She thinks if she goes away, she'll miss her chance and she's desperate to get out of the Rossville Flats. So, I wondered if you want to go with me. Please say yes. I need some decent company on the trip."

"Heavens Siobhan, that's some luck you've had. But it's about time. When are you thinking we'd be going?"

"May."

I took my chance to bring her up to date.

"Before I reply, I want to tell you, Connor and I are getting married this Christmas. He's going to move over here in the summer. It'll be a bit of a squeeze to fit in the trip, but I'll talk to everyone tonight because I'd love to go with you. What was the competition?"

She told me it was to do with the local tourist board in Newfoundland. She'd apparently found out about it in a travel agency when she was booking a flight.

She ended with, "I'm really pleased to hear about your wedding, but please try to come. We can do some wedding planning while we're away."

I called her back the next day. Connor had encouraged me to go, so I agreed, dusted off my passport and gave thanks my parents had agreed to pay for the

wedding. That gave me some cash to play
with.

For me, May was reasonable timing. I
didn't want to start looking for a
place for us to stay in Dumfries until
your dad came over in the summer. And
a trip to Canada was too good an opportunity to turn down.

And that was how the trip came about—
completely out of the blue.

In the next phone call, I informed Siobhan, she was to be a bridesmaid. I'd
been nervous about asking her only
months after Aidan's… but she agreed
with no hesitation. You see, we were
getting back to the rhythm of our old
friendship.

During the trip, I gave her the basics.
It was to be a simple wedding. I wanted
two bridesmaids, Siobhan and Geraldine, and we agreed the trip to Canada
would be an opportunity to discuss
dresses, flowers etcetera.

*[Note: We were in danger of going into the weeds again
while she went into the details of bride's maid dress col-
ours, flowers and so I butted in at this point.]*

A.J.: How did she seem at the time
Rose: As I said, it felt like we were
getting back to normal, but she

certainly wasn't the energetic friend who would once have given me a list of conditions before agreeing to wear a bridesmaid's dress. And when we met in Glasgow to set off for Canada, I was shocked, her eyes seemed lost in her head, her mood definitely subdued. But I didn't expect much else. On the day, she wore her hair pulled back tightly from her face. No earrings, or eye makeup. And during our stay in Newfoundland, she took daily solitary walks on the rugged coastline of the island as I read wedding magazines. We both got a bit of what we needed.

For me, I really appreciated the rest. The coastline of Newfoundland reminded us of our homes. Like both of our homelands, the hills were green, the cliffs fell away to the sea, and the people had a curiously Irish-sounding accent. The locals waved their hellos as we walked around.

I definitely felt like we restored the line of communication between us, like before the event with Aidan and time had separated us.

[Note: "And what about after the trip," I asked—it was important to miss no detail of Siobhan's life and her demeanour.]

Rose: Over the next few months Siobhan called at the farm no more than a couple of times. It was understandable. She was scheduled to complete her master's degree after the wedding and then planned to stay on in Glasgow as her department was being commissioned to help with some new inner-city redevelopment plans. She said she saw this as her launch into a PhD, but that she might take a break from academia for a while.

For me, the bonus in her news was Siobhan would not be returning to live in Derry any time soon.

I probably don't need to go into the wedding in any great detail. You've seen the video and photographs. Suffice to say, and thanks mostly to the Irish contingent, the rain didn't dampen our spirits. You can see Siobhan was right there in the photos, smiling. We insisted her mother, Mary, come over with Connor's mum and so the whole of the family with Wee Patrick as best man were caught up in the record of the day.

I felt Siobhan and me were turning a corner, but it has to be said that hovering in the background was the thought it was less than a month to the first anniversary of Aidan's….

To keep the timeline straight for you, my grandpa and grandma were danced and feted and judging by the slight flush in their cheeks, got a little bit drunk. The wedding of Grandpa's 'little treasure', as he used to call me, would be their last appearance at a large family gathering. They died the next year, and within a few months of each other. Grandpa died first, of a heart attack and it was found only weeks later Grandma had a tumour on her lung. She said she had no wish to have surgery and died peacefully sedated. She was laid to rest with her husband in the week they would have celebrated their golden wedding anniversary.

Your dad joined other members of the family in bearing them on their shoulders and taking each in turn to the family grave site in Dalbeattie.

Your grandmother, Peggy, received a part of her parent's legacy and decided to help her four children plan their futures. Your dad and I added our share of this to our savings. We were staying with Walter and Peggy and working for a down payment on a house. And for the sake of rounding off the story, your dad's mother died of a stroke within a year of our wedding and only six months after leading her daughter Maxine up the aisle to marry a Newry man. After a small bequest was given to her sister Mary, Connor and Maxine inherited their mother's small estate. This included the house she had lived in all her married life. Maxine agreed to buy Connor's share and two years after our wedding, we moved into the house we are sitting in. And not too long after, you arrived.

A.J.: It sounds like there was a load of sadness hovering around for quite a while. Did it feel like that to you? And did it ever occur to you that she might have felt jealous of how perfectly things were working out for you?

Rose: If Siobhan was jealous, I didn't notice it.

[Note: Right after she said that, I watched her rerunning events of that time in her head. I almost believe that I stirred something she had been unaware of—she quickly got back onto the track she had been on.]

Rose: You asked if the atmosphere around us was sad? Between your dad and me, we never wanted to dwell on the role the death of loved ones played in laying the foundation we have and we wanted. You must have noticed, each year on our wedding anniversary, we have a family party with music and song, but on January 31, we acknowledged the passing of all the people we loved. On that day there's always a vase of red roses and white chrysanthemums on the table in the dining room, and we make sure it is a day of peace in the house. No cross words. No what-ifs. No regrets.

[*Note: The energy in the room lagged, and I stretched to get some oxygen circulating in my body. I wanted to get to the end of this and so forced myself to pick up the energy in my voice as I asked*] How were things with Siobhan after the wedding?

Rose: As regards to Siobhan, there wasn't regular contact—the odd phone call, maybe a couple of visits from her after we moved in here. It took six months after your birth for Siobhan to call. I was a little surprised she left it so long, but I knew she'd been going to Australia and the U.S. from time to time—some paper she was writing.
"Lots of Irish people in those places," she remarked to us as she handed out gifts she'd brought us from Australia

where she'd been a guest lecturer at a
conference in Melbourne. In a few years
She'd turned into quite the academic.
But the real surprise wasn't the visit
itself. It was that with her was a marine biologist called Cameron. She told
us he was going to be starting a work
project on the West Coast of Scotland.
I think we must have looked slack-jawed
when they both turned up at the door,
but Siobhan launched herself at us and
carried on a fast-paced commentary regardless of how we must have looked.
She was animated, lively, and most of
all, verbose.

Cameron was a short-head taller than
she and had a serious look about him.
Apart from his work in marine biology,
we learned he was a part time officer
in an army reserve regiment. I was
careful not to let my jaw drop any further.

Dad and I were pointedly told on the
visit we were the only family members
she was telling about Cameron's military connections. She pleaded for neither of us to mention a word to her
family. I'm almost certain the pair of
us carried on looking dumb and confused
for the entire two-hour visit. I made
tea but your dad didn't come through to

the kitchen, so I didn't get to react to the news until they left.

Then I said, "What in the name of God was that? I didn't recognise that person"

Your dad replied, "She will never cease to amaze me. I could never have imagined her marrying a British soldier in my wildest dreams. I'm going to have to sit down before I fall down."

"You can't tell me this doesn't seem a bit weird to you. I'd always assumed Siobhan had a hostile attitude to the British, and particularly the British authorities around the day Aidan was shot. And so, I wondered how she'd been able to separate all of that and Cameron's military connection. She's not telling Mary or Brendan, so she obviously sees how others will react.

The only thing I could imagine is that Cameron's offered her something missing in her life. Something with more pull than the grief. I wish I could have asked her about it, and that was part of the problem. I didn't know if she'd let me in me in so I could find out what was going on in her head. And I worried about her. Because unless she'd made friends I didn't know about, who else would she have to talk to about this momentous event. The only hope I could cling to was that finding Cameron would be the beginning of a new life for her. A tiny little part of me thought, God, I hope she's not planning to murder the man in his bed."

[Note: Interesting thing for her to think!]

I remember how worried your dad looked and he butted in to make a point. "You do realise her state of mind isn't the only problem, don't you? That's not the reason she's asking us to keep it secret."
I must have looked a bit vague because he faced me and took me by the shoulders. "You do know what they do to Catholic Derry girls who go with British soldiers don't you?"
The dawning crept over me, and I felt sick—women, hair cropped, smeared with tar or shit of some kind, roped to lampposts for all to jeer at. And they were probably the lucky ones. Some would have disappeared, or their dead bodies tossed onto their parent's doorstep. I got his point.
A.J.: When did you see them again?
Rose: I only remember the pair of them visiting us once and Siobhan asked us

then to be the witnesses at their civil wedding about six months later.

Young Walter and Geraldine took care of you on the farm while your dad and I went to Glasgow. We were the only family there on either side.

A.J.: Did you manage to find out any more about her state of mind?

Rose: As we checked into our hotel room the day before the wedding, Siobhan looked at me gave me a big smile, like from our St. Andrew's days, and said, "I'm marrying a British soldier. I can't believe it. I bet you can't either. You must know how I felt about things in Northern Ireland but maybe not so much how I dealt with it inside. There's a word you hear in Ireland you don't hear nearly as much anywhere else--bitterness. Ireland is a country drowning in bitterness and the people can taste it in their mouths every time they are wronged, and it creeps easily into our conversations. Our minds flash on everything from the famine, through the Croke Park massacre to the civil war, and that sourness comes up and warps our thinking.

She went on quickly, hardly pausing for breath. "I do want to apologise, Rose. I was probably a real pain in the arse

the past while. I could have said more
to my friends, but I bottled things up.
Completely illogical, right?"

*[Note: Mum looked at me, maybe for affirmation. She
was describing ways I could understand. But I kept quiet.
I didn't want to disturb the flow of what she was saying.]*

Rose: Siobhan explained more to me
about her state of mind, saying it was
the very lack of drama in Cameron's
life that resonated with her—because it
was allowing her to regain the part of
her life she'd worked for, building
from her time at university and had
been hard for her to keep hold of. She
was very clear the anger over Aidan was
a real burden she was glad to lay down.
I got that straight from her, A.J. I
completely understood where she was
coming from.
And although she didn't say so in so
many words, I think she'd been completely honest with Cameron and how it
was for an Irish Catholic woman to
marry a British soldier, how it was way
beyond the pale, an act of treachery as
far as they were concerned. What she
did say was she thought the best strat-
egy had been to surprise Brendan and
her mother with a ring already on her

finger and no prior warning of Lieutenant Cameron.

She convinced me she'd moved on to a
new phase. They had already gone to
Melbourne together when he was on a
tour of duty there, and although I
didn't see her often, I got the distinct feeling over those couple of
hours she'd warmed up to her work
friends again after a period of staying
aloof.

I think I'm remembering these conversations in the correct order. Right after the wedding service, we were sitting together again, your dad and Cameron had gone to the bar in the hotel,
and we talked. She went back to losing
Aidan and how it was the worst thing in
the world, but then how one day she
realised being desperately lonely came
a close second to that pain.

She said she and Cameron had talked a
lot about Aidan's death at first and
he'd been sympathetic. They agreed
never to talk about his soldier pals
and if they were ever on the streets of
Derry. She knew he had never personally
been posted to Northern Ireland.

I remember she said something like,
"I'd like for the bastards who killed
Aidan to get what they deserve, but

Cameron didn't kill Aidan any more than you or I did. Now, as far as I'm concerned, I've been given a gift, I can set my eyes on the future again, the first time in a long while."

She sounded genuinely excited about the future. She must have told me a dozen times what a really good man he was and how he had saved her life.

A.J.: How did you feel when she was telling you this?

Rose: I could never have imagined Siobhan saying those words six months before, but I was so happy she was getting the opportunity to find some peace and happiness. I decided to move on with her. Your dad and I fell into step, accepting what we saw at face value.

[Note: Mum looked at me, but only briefly. I gave her no room to find emotion on my face. I didn't want to give her a route into her usual route to a safe cocoon where nothing could touch her belief in her friend and their friendship. If she had any doubt in what she was saying, I thought it important it came from her not me.]

Rose: I did question her a bit. At one point, I asked her if she was really okay? And I asked if she would tell me if something was wrong.

189

"I have to admit it all seems a bit quick," I said, I'm not sure at what point in the evening I said it, but I can remember what she said next fairly clearly, and if she was annoyed, she didn't show it.

She said, "I know what it looks like, but my life's been chaos, and I mean the whole of my life not just since Aidan was murdered. Now, I want some peace with someone who's steady and dependable. I realise Cameron's hard to get to know, but when you do, you'll find someone who's sure where he's headed in life. He makes plans and carries them through. And he's very thoughtful. At last, I've got a man I can rely on. I'm used to men who depend on me. Men I can't save, no matter how hard I try—my dad, our Brendan and Aidan. You see, Cameron doesn't need me to save him."

"Well then," I answered, "Cherish what you have. You've got my backing."

A.J.: What about the rest of the family?

Rose: She went through with the plan to visit her mother and brother in Derry with the marriage a *fait accompli*, Cameron being warned to keep his military status to himself. As he seemed not to be a man to court trouble, he became complicit in keeping Siobhan's life in Northern Ireland at arm's length and to visit there only when necessary. The occasions to do so, as far as I could tell, were few and far between.

Your dad didn't stop reminding me the reaction in Derry that could very well happen if it was discovered Rose had married a British soldier.

"No one will care if he's just part time. So, let's be sure it goes no further than ourselves." I could tell how deadly serious he was, and I was always careful even in talking to my own family lest the secret be accidentally revealed.

So we didn't even talk to Brendan or any of Dad's cousin's about it

A.J.: Did Aidan's death ever come up again with Siobhan?

The pair visited from time to time. Cameron often worked on the Solway Firth, and they came to stay with us when they were in the area.

A.J.: And how were things with Cameron over this time?

Rose: I can't say I ever warmed to him. His coolness unsettled me. I would find myself searching his face for, I don't know what, and I would spend time after every visit talking to your dad. Cameron wasn't his favourite subject, and so those conversations never went very far.

[Note: We took a little break at this point – Dad had come into kitchen, he refilled our water glasses. He then he sat, mostly reading the paper, in a chair at the far end of the table and waited for me to get back to my spot.]

A.J.: What were we saying about Cameron?
Connor: Cameron was an odd duck.
Rose: So, let's get down to the last piece of the puzzle.
I remember the day, almost a year after their wedding, I was running around the garden. I remember you were chasing me, and your dad came through the gate as the phone rang. He picked up the call in the kitchen.
Connor: It was from Cameron calling from the west coast of Vancouver Island. With little build up or ceremony, he blurted out that Siobhan had been killed by a gunman. A bullet through her chest the previous morning while she was out jogging alone. I asked what they had been doing in Canada, and he said he'd been consulting with the Canadian forces on something or other and

presenting a paper at a symposium at the University of Victoria. Siobhan had gone with him for a bit of a holiday.

He gave the impression the call had to be brief, but he didn't say why. He said there were no suspects, or clues to why it had happened.

I asked how he was doing, and he jumped over the question and said, "I'm coming back with the body in the next few days. I'll be fine but could you give me the phone number of her mother in Derry?" And added, "the police still have all her stuff."

I wondered if he would even have called if he didn't need to, but I gave him the information he wanted and asked to be kept informed of the funeral arrangements. Then, shocked and bewildered, I went into the garden and asked your mother to sit beside me at the picnic table. You were only two. You toddled over. We sat you between us and held hands.

Rose: Just over two weeks later we were back in church in Derry

Cameron had agreed to Mary's pleas to have her buried in Ireland. I was shocked Brendan was not at the funeral. In fact, Mary's one remaining child, who was now a roadie with some band or other, was drunk in a bar in the centre of the town. People were saying he couldn't stand the idea of burying another sibling.

Mary stood beside Cameron at the graveside with me on her other side. I took her icy fingers into the palms of my own hands.

She said, "Rose, what happened. Do you know what happened?"

Your dad squeezed between herself and Cameron and wrapped an arm around her. He said, "I don't think anyone knows for sure."

A.J.: How was Cameron at the service?

Rose: As much as I remember, Cameron stared ahead and then suddenly, with his head bowed and no word to anyone, he walked away to his car.

Connor: I didn't go after him, figuring every man had a right to grieve in his own way—even though it seemed incredibly unfeeling toward his late wife's mother.

I called him a few times after the funeral to find out if there had been any updates on the case, but the call was always brief and the answer always 'no'. And I would phone Aunt Mary so she would know someone was keeping vigil with her.

A.J.: You never heard anything else about the death and you're sure no one was charged?

Connor: I only spoke to him when I called those few times over a period of about four years. After that, he must have changed his phone number because I could never get through to him.

A.J.: I did a search on the Net and couldn't see any reports the murder was solved. But I did find this.

[Note: I showed them a print of a wedding picture taken in 2001. It was Cameron and an Elaine Kennedy, married in Ayr—they both took a look at the picture.]

Connor: Well, he never told us.

Rose: I know we were only connected through Siobhan but still…. You'd think he could at least have let us know. I'd have sent a card for sure.

A.J.: Do you have any clue where he lives now?

Conner: No, none. Why?

A.J.: Completion. He has a bit of the story no one else has. There's a gap somewhere and he might have clues about who had decided to kill her—and if it was intentional rather than an accident.

Rose: Don't you think it was likely to have been the random act of a mad man. And don't you think he'd have told the authorities if he had the slightest idea who killed his wife?

[Note: *I looked at Mum over my glasses. It was a look I reserve for putting people on the spot who have said something stupid. After a few seconds, a penny seemed dropped with her.*]

Rose: You surely don't think he killed his own wife after eleven months of marriage.
A.J.: Did you ever wonder?

[Note: *The two spoke over the top of each other.*]

Rose: Never. A.J., you have a real wicked mind...
Connor: Well, of course it's only natural to think... But he would have been the first one they'd have looked at. They always look at the husband.
Rose: Yes, right, so he must've had an alibi. He was working that day on the base out there... Plenty of people would have seen him
A.J.: Maybe, but I'd still like to see the man face to face.

Connor: Well, you'll need to dig around
to find him. We can't help you there.

[Note: It was left like that, abruptly. Neither of them wanting to accept my doubts and me feeling they were being annoyingly naïve. I believe we skirted around a row I was too tired or squeamish to embark on.]

END OF TRANSCRIPT

The next morning, as promised, I helped Mum in the garden. The activity mostly took place in silence. I didn't mind it. She kept her distance from me and bustled about close to the back door.

Her last gesture of the weekend was to hand me a pile of clean clothes, folded and ready to put in my bag. It's hard to hold onto annoyance with someone who does your laundry for you, but some how I managed it.

I know how to read her. The active coolness was meant to convey annoyance, cancelling out the token of the laundry folding. I like to think I rose above it. My morning-brain hadn't found anything else solid enough to challenge her.

We parted with polite pecks to the cheek. It was cool, mechanical, and I felt the distance between us had opened, if possible, even wider, than before. All of this because I asked questions about why Siobhan needed to die and at whose hand. Rose had retreated to maintaining a rigid mind-set I had not really managed to penetrate on any meaningful level.

Dad wasn't teaching that morning, but he went into school for a while and he picked me up in time for the 12:30 train.

"Well, did you get what your expected?" He asked.

"Not sure. There's a lot of Siobhan lying hidden somewhere. Not sure if Mum and you have plumbed the depths of the mystery yet." I needed to buy time before I talked anything else through with him.

Instead of waiting for him question me, I jumped in with a diversion, "But at least I kept Mum away from asking whether I'd found 'anyone special' yet."

He took my lead and followed me out of the Siobhan quagmire. As we got out of the car at Lockerbie station, I said I'd keep him updated, and I had one last question as he was getting my bag out of the back of the car.

"Are you still in touch with Brendan?" I asked.

"I've a mobile phone number for him and I think he hangs about the Creggan estate in Derry. More, I'm not sure. I think Wee Patrick sees him once in a while."

"Can you email me the number you have for him."

"Sure. But don't be going over there without telling me."

"Don't worry."

He brought me in for a hug. "That's a completely stupid thing to say to me, peace agreement or no peace agreement."

I didn't blame him for his concern, after all the last time he'd lived in Ireland it was a dangerous place for a stranger.

Then I broke with caution and said, "Dad, did you ever wonder who killed her?"

"'Course I did, but what could I do from over here. Grab a gun and go looking on the West Coast of Canada? And Cameron was the one who was her next of kin. We relied on him for information, and we got precious little."

"But didn't you think, no matter where she died, it might be something to do with Ireland?"

"Again, how would I go about doing anything about that? I had nothing to do with the Provos and even if I had the notion, if I messed about with that crowd, I could have put you and your mother at risk."

I didn't want to let it go. "Did you ever even talk to Brendan about it?"

"No. He was moving in different circles. For all intents and purposes, he was missing in action."

"So. What do you think now?"

He got into the car, opened the window, and clicked on his seat belt.

"I don't let myself think. It safest."

"Does Mum talk about it?"

"No and I want you to leave her be now. We've helped out. Let that be the end of it."

I stepped back from the car. He'd slipped into his usual role of family shock-absorber.

Always the man to part on a light-hearted note, he looked at me, changed the subject and said, "Well, have you found anyone special yet?"

I rolled my eyes and waved as he drove away, pleased I'd let him have the last word.

Aware of where I stood with my bag at my feet, a sense of irony went through my mind. There I was examining deaths rooted in The Troubles, standing within half a mile of where a plane ripped through the small Scottish market town in 1988, allegedly blown up in mid-air by a bomb planted by a radical Islamic terrorist from Libya. Death seemingly touched down randomly, that day, killing people on the road, at a petrol station and in their houses. Two causes set so geographically apart—Ireland and Libya—and yet in in the world of terror, so politically proximate. My chest tightened thinking of the horror of those days when violence took ordinary people and scarred families in this town.

When I turned away from the road, I crossed through the Victorian station. My footsteps echoed off the wooden floorboards as I passed onto the Edinburgh platform. I looked both ways. How many of the people living a stone's throw from here still had nightmares and remembered the months when first responders from all over the south of Scotland and investigators from all over the world walked along the granite streets—needing food, beds and laundry services from a town ill-equipped for the trauma? Anger was easily accessible.

I started as suddenly the train to Waverley Station pulled in. And given my anger, I didn't even have the pleasure of slamming the door at my back. My mood was heavy, dark, with…. what?

Anger. At what? With whom?

9. Night Visitors

Source: From memory
Time Reference: 1972-1977

Edinburgh washed over me as soon as I arrived on the train from Lockerbie. I was back on familiar ground. As I passed through Waverly, I grabbed a coffee to accompany the sandwich Mum had packed for me and handed to me by Dad. Before I departed, I called at the office for a few hours work on the job I actually get paid for.

I was waylaid by the political editor as I walked in. He wanted me on the Liberal's Party members within the UK's coalition government. I told him I'd get right to it and flopped down at my desk.

He did ask how the 'family thing' was going? I told him it was slow and that I would take a while to get to grips with a few loose ends. But he didn't seem to worry I'd be distracted by it, and I didn't put him wise.

Booting up my desktop, I printed out all the names of the present Cabinet and close Liberal Party advisers—called SPADS for short—stuffed it into my bag and then searched online for information on Cameron, the part time soldier, and husband of the late Siobhan. He must be on record somewhere, I thought.

Eureka!

As I walked home, I phoned my inside-source at the Scottish Office and she gave me the low-down on who was in, and who was out at Downing Street. The general opinion was Nick Clegg, the Liberal Deputy Prime Minister, was likeable, and unusually knowledgeable by virtue of his years of service in Brussels. Given this, I didn't hold out hope of gaining an original insight into some foible or other he possessed. But I'd only just begun, and I had enough from her to line up my research project for the next few days. I wasn't getting energised by it, probably because I understood the assignment was no more than a piece to file in case it was needed later. It didn't need to take up much space in my brain.

Good news given my mind had been taken over by the weekend events and deciding when I would work on the transcripts of my recorded notes.

I landed in my flat on Elm Row around 7:00 and looked in the fridge. It would need to be Pot Noodles for supper. After staying at the parent's place over the weekend, it was going to be a bit of a cold-turkey withdrawal from nutritious food. And the dishes in the sink, several days old were disgusting.

I grabbed the Sundays from the door mat and settled down to do a cover to cover read. It was a weekly journalistic duty. I put my feet up after I had eaten and finished a beer. The buzzer sounded from downstairs, and I picked up the entrance phone.

"Henry here."

"Come up." What's this about, I wondered.

When he got upstairs, he apologised for coming by without warning and explained he was visiting his kids in Edinburgh who stayed with his now ex-wife, Faye, and it seemed like a good opportunity to come by and catch up. I took his coat and placed it over the back of a kitchen chair. He accepted a beer, and I took a second can to keep him company. We went over to the comfy seats. He looked tired and said he'd walked for miles with the kids, mostly around shops. He had no bags with him, and I assumed the shopping was his payment of the requisite divorced-dad guilt money. He was, after all, the guilty party that brought his marriage to an end. Some fling with a work colleague.

Divorce wasn't sitting well with him. He'd put on weight, his cheeks were red, his Adam's apple was nestling somewhere inside a fat neck. He had a generally bloated look. I flashed on earlier memories of a lean, keen teacher at the front of my Maths class in high school. Things had changed. He was pensioned off from full-time teaching—doing something for a few hours a week at an adult education centre with twenty somethings trying to redeem their lives after misspent teenage years. At the same time, he was writing a book on William Wallace, the early Scottish warrior, or so he told me. He said he hoped hanging out with me for a bit would rub off and gift him energy to get into the project with more gusto.

"So, how's the writing going," I asked.

"I'd written three chapters, and today on the train, I deleted the whole lot. Rubbish."

No one argues with writers. There's no point in saying, 'I hoped you saved them, they probably weren't that bad.' I nodded, one writer to another understanding the frustrations. I assumed he'd called by for this kind of chat, but I had the overwhelming sense of a depressed man looking for company and to share his misery.

"I've been home to Dumfries. Spent the weekend working on my project."

"What's that?" he asked.

"I'm trying to piece together what happened to Siobhan and how her story fits in with the family."

I got him another beer from the fridge and offered him a vodka which he accepted, tilting slightly as he stood to follow me to the kitchen. I prepared myself to have him sleep on the sofa.

"I knew about Siobhan. She was my first real love. But... she'd have none of me."

"Do you mind if I record this? You might say something I'll want to remember." It could have been considered a joke and he laughed, maybe at the unfamiliar idea of being useful.

"Sure," he said.

I got up, switched on the recorder, and brought it over, placing it on the arm of my chair.

TRANSCRIPT – CONVERSATION WITH HENRY (UNCLE)
A.J.: Tell me, when did you last see Siobhan?

Henry: It was before she married Cameron. She must've been visiting Rose. So it would've been '75 or '76. I can't remember if you were born or not, but neither of us were married at that point. I was seeing your aunt Faye off and on. Truth be told, I believe I was still hoping Siobhan might change her mind, run into my arms like in one of those rom com movies.

A.J.: How did she seem to you?

Henry: You know, I'd been worried about her after Aidan was killed. She got thin and hard looking. The few times I saw her, she wouldn't meet my eyes or crack a joke. Understandable, but I regretted that I could never get close enough to offer any comfort, and of course, she never came to me.

[Note: he was beginning to slur his words and clunked the ice cubes around in his glass. He sat back, but I didn't want him to drift off into sleep—not yet.]

A.J.: I don't know if I really under-stand what she felt about our family. What d'you think?

Henry: One night, ages back, we were sitting in a bar in Dumfries. She must've been visiting with your parents, and I'd got her to come out with me for a drink. I don't remember exactly when, but those occasions were rare, so I remember them. I don't know how we got started on the subject, but I remember her saying, "You know, there are times when I hate Rose."

I was shocked, they'd always seemed so close, but she went on, and I was willing to try to make sense of what she was saying.

She continued, "So far, I'd always felt lucky to be born into a caring brood that had moved from a cramped two-up, two-down house to a new flat in the Bogside, a place teeming with mates. We ran wild among concrete pillars onto the grass and among hiding places in the bushes."

She was opening up about childish memories and I stupidly felt things might be taking a turn for the better, for her and me that is.

She went on, "My father died when I was young, but I had a doting mother, and two brothers. Ma worked to support us, and we were fed and clothed. St. Columba's School nurtured my mind up to a point. However, I wasn't stupid or naïve, I knew other kids came from greater privilege and wouldn't have to rely on grants and part time jobs to pay their way through university. But

I imagined them in cold homes without a mother to sing to them, to tell them they were brilliant, and to study hard to get on. That way, I didn't feel in the least deprived."

[Note: I gave him another small shot of Vodka trying to keep things social, I felt I was getting gold from him.]

Henry: She carried on. "That was until I met the unsettling Rose at St. Andrews University as the 60s drew to a close. Your family's background wasn't so hugely wealthy that I felt intimidated, but it was a far cry from the Bogside. It was only after I was drawn into your mother's life. I learned to ride a pony. It was during the times spent in her company I could walk around the streets without fear of being hit in the crossfire of bricks or bullets. Until I moved to St. Andrews, I'd never been in a town's main shopping area where there were no barricades to deter car bombers, and no police bag searches.
"I didn't discuss the characters of the eighteenth-century Enlightenment when I was home in the Bogside. It wasn't in Northern Ireland I settled on a career in social planning, even though it was the Bogside that showed me the dark side of planned housing.

"And I was so enthusiastic about Rose visiting my hometown in the year we graduated—even though the place was a tip, with makeshift barriers built by the young boys and others by the army practically outside our door. But, in my gut, I thought it was important for her education to be rounded-off with a dose of Derry reality."

I remember her laughing at her own wit and I joined in. Can't think why. I remember that time so well, and I certainly didn't want Rose going over there for a visit. Anyway, the only other thing I remember from that night was Siobhan finishing up saying, "Any thoughts I may have had about her making unfavourable comparisons between her granite farmhouse and my family's council flat were unfounded. She was a good friend. She charmed both my mother and cousin Connor when they met her. I thought she was a great girl. It was only the mean side of me that ever thought badly of her and that was only after she died, and I wandered what she might have gotten herself into. But I didn't come up with the foggiest notion of what that could have been. After all, she was settled as Glasgow. She seemed committed to her studies and her career. Any curiosity eventually faded away."

[Note: I took his glass away because he was starting to drop off, but the action woke him up with a start. He got a tissue out of his trouser pocket to wipe at his mouth.]

A.J.: When was the last time you saw her in person?

Henry: I think Aidan had already been killed.

A.J.: What do remember about that time?

Henry: Not much, she called at my flat in Dumfries and we had something to eat. She had an overnight case with her. Travelling light. Curiously, she left without it.

A.J.: What was in it?

Henry: She had left it sitting in my hallway. I opened it but it was empty.

A.J.: Did you make anything of it?

Henry: It was a bit strange, and Faye quizzed me, especially when she heard it was Siobhan's. She even phoned her in a snit, probably hoping she'd catch me in a lie. But Siobhan told her the lock was acting up and to keep it or give it to a charity shop—she had a new one. I didn't attach any major importance to it, and it never came up again.

A.J: Do you have a theory about why Siobhan was murdered.

Henry: I've thought of it quite a bit and I kept coming back to Cameron. I met him once, and he was a strange one for sure. I Couldn't see what she saw in him.

A.J.: But why would he do it, d'you think?

Henry: Maybe something to do with him being a soldier, and her being a girl from Derry.

A.J.: But why would he have married her in the first place if that was an issue?

Henry: And I also thought she was maybe pregnant and that forced their hand. But obviously that wasn't the case. In the end, I decided she just fancied the whole touring around and not needing to be settled like she would if she married someone like a teacher. She really was a load of fun and she'd already got a taste for travelling.

A.J.: So, in your version, she marries him for fun and adventure, he agrees for whatever reason, and then kills her because he regrets marrying someone from Northern Ireland.

Henry: Put like that, I can see how there are some holes in the logic of the story, but at least it is an

```
explanation. The alternative is nada,
a complete mystery.
A.J.: Fair enough. But if you think of
anything else, shoot me off an email.
In the meantime, get your head down
here. I'll grab you a blanket.
```

END OF TRANSCRIPT

After I switched off the lights, I got into bed and tossed and turned a bit. Henry had given me information about Siobhan's attitude to my mum that blew a hole in the unspoiled sisterly-love version of the relationship my Mum would have me believe. Sleep wasn't coming and I sat up, bashed at my pillows, and switched on the bedside lamp. I tried to read but couldn't concentrate and drifted back to reviewing the weekend.

I knew, with absolute certainty, I could eliminate Mum and Dad as being suspects in Siobhan's death. For me, that only left Cameron or some unknown hitman. I should, I thought, include Brendan, her older brother. Maybe he'd found out about her husband's background in the British army. I suppose it was possible that it would have been expected of him to commit an honour killing. I still hadn't cleared up why my parents were reluctant to dig into the circumstances of her death and two possibilities remained unsettled. Firstly, that they had a suspect in mind and were unwilling to see him or her brought to justice or secondly, that they harboured a suspicion that Siobhan was involved in something nefarious that led to her death. In the latter case, they might have thought it best that no one rummaged around in her background and to let her death fade until it was a distant memory. I had to face the unpleasant truth my parents were party to a miscarriage of justice related to the most atrocious of crimes known to society. In that regard, I was no further forward.

I'm not sure when I transitioned from resting my eyes to falling asleep, and at what point I was disturbed by the appearance of a delicate figure standing at the foot if the bed.

She had long dark hair, and I could see through what I would describe as a floaty nightdress to the room behind her. I stared, voiceless, waiting for her to do something or to explain herself.

She went straight into what she had come to say.

"When the gunman came for me, it was a shock. I was out running and there was a moment. Not quite a second. Not even half a second, when I felt the heat but not the pain. I sensed against my cheek, the coarse turf which clung thinly to the gravel below. The sea boomed. It filled my ears—nature's muffler.

"A lifetime of experience would have told him there was no need for him to come over to check his handiwork. In the morning light, not a single shadow fell over me. My body shuddered and my mind lapsed to the primal, the essential. I drifted back to my mother's kitchen in Derry. To the moment when singing a song of collective national pain became a pursuit that consumed all around me."

Then the vision started to sing and drifted away. I only just managed to make out the words from the song I'd heard my father sing.

...My heart strove the two between
The old love and the new love... *

I woke suddenly and looked at the clock. The whole incident couldn't have taken more than a couple of seconds. I gave my head a shake, wiped my palms on the bottom sheet and decided I was desperately sleep deprived. Maybe I was conjuring up bits of conversations I'd heard as a kid and putting them together in a way my subconscious could make sense of.

I got up to go to the bathroom and did a mental shrug—my ghostly apparition wasn't all that original—all floaty and ethereal—and it touched on both the fact of her murder and the culture of the time. Was the murder centered there? Should I look no further?

In the morning, after Henry left, in the midst of the smell of unwashed socks and beer breath, I recorded what I remembered of the dream and took myself off to work. As soon as I set off on foot I thought, 'so if you go on with this, you have to face the fact that the next person or people you interview could be a killer. Way different from chatting to Mummy and Daddy.'

10. Cameron

Source: Transcript of interview with Cameron 2011
Time Reference: 1975 – 1977

I was a bit early, but that was my choice. It was two weeks after Dumfries that I waited in Green Beans, a coffee shop and lunch place inside Queens Street Station, in the centre of Glasgow. I wanted to centre myself before he arrived. I'd typed up all the transcripts from the weekend with my parents, and now, I thought I had as much information as it was possible to glean out of the material. Now, there were two more players in my sights. Cameron was number one.

He'd been fairly easy to find, living on Mull, an island off the west coast. Today he was passing through the city on his way to give a guest lecture, and I'd volunteered to take the train from Edinburgh to make the meeting as easy as possible on him.

My recorder was live but hidden. I sat. I was freshy showered and had my best black jeans on. After all, he was a military man, and I thought it best to create the impression of a person who was reasonably together. The surroundings hummed with quiet conversation, piped soft rock played in the background. Everything was clean, easy to wipe down, a functional place for travellers to pass through or, as in my case, to meet up with others.

Cameron should have the head-and-shoulders picture of me I'd emailed. As I'd been about three years old the last time we met, it seemed a good idea to give him a something better than a childhood image from deep in his memory to work with.

I hadn't mentioned to him I was a journalist, and to keep my head clear of any unwanted advice they were bound to offer, I didn't give my parents notice of the meeting. There was also the matter of my being an inexperienced investigative journalist. Nerves meant it was a constant effort to keep my feet from tapping. After all, he might interpret my nervousness as shiftiness.

I had my cover story sorted out and now I need only to keep still and wait.

He walked in at the same time as three random women and looked around. I put my phone on the table and raised my hand in the air. He came right over, holdall and a briefcase, one in each hand, no hat covering fair short-cropped hair that would probably have been wavy if it'd been given a chance to grow.

216

I stood and we shook hands awkwardly as he simultaneously placed his luggage on the floor beside the table.

His neck, arms and shoulders were bulky and his grip intimidating. He was a man built to take care of himself, and possibly others.

"Aidan," I said. There was a moment when he missed a beat, no doubt the name catching him somewhere internally, but he quickly got on with pumping my arm for a few more seconds.

"Cameron."

I tried to quickly place his accent—northeast England, slightly corrupted by spending a lot of time in Scotland.

I offered to buy him coffee and a snack. When I came back from the counter with coffee and muffins, he didn't waste time making the most of what I put down on the table.

"You say you're putting together an album for a surprise Christmas present for your parents," he said, stirring milk into his drink and taking a tentative sip of the hot liquid. He burned his lip. Could it be he was nervous too?

I went on, giving him a chance to mop his mouth and chin. "Yeah, it's a surprise for them and, as I said in my email, I wondered if you had any photos. Plus, I want to get the section I'm writing up on Siobhan absolutely right. So, I thought if we chatted, you would have some extra bits I don't know about."

It was a thin story, but three weeks before, I'd got a face-to-face with a Scottish Government Minister on less, and I'd gone out of my way to come and meet the man here in Glasgow—that should surely get me some points. At the very least, I had hoped his curiosity would win. It seemed to have worked.

217

I turned my lap top around and showed him the picture of my mum and Siobhan the day after their graduation in St. Andrews. He squinted at it slightly but didn't linger for more than a couple of seconds. Then he looked at the wall over my shoulder.

Maybe to break the silence or to hurry things along, he pulled out from the inside of his waterproof jacket an envelope and emptied the contents onto the table. There were two wedding pictures, all showing my parents with Siobhan and him at a registry office. He offered no embellishment beyond what could be seen on the face of the photos.

"You don't want to keep these?" I said already spreading them over the table and looking for anything I might want to question.

"You're okay. I've got others."

"Thanks."

"If you've got questions, ask away." There was clearly going to be no small talk about football or the weather between us.

"My parents gave me a vague version of how you and Siobhan got together and how they came to meet you, but I'd like to hear it from your side. You probably have some details they don't. Maybe a funny anecdote or two about the wedding or anything else you can think of."

I pointed to a shot of Siobhan and Mum holding onto each other both dressed in smart dresses and jackets—no bouquets, simple buttonholes of white roses.

I asked, "Is there something I can surprise them with."

"I don't know about that. You can see we were all smiles" He pointed to a picture of the couple with my Mum and Dad. I thought to myself how good looking my dad was. Not for the first time I wondered if I got most of my genes from Robert the red-haired soldier, but without the red hair.

If Cameron was feeling any kind of emotion, strong or otherwise, it wasn't showing. I watched him carefully as he spoke.

[Note: See notes attached to the transcript below.]

TRANSCRIPT – INTERVIEW WITH CAMERON

Cameron: It was a flight from Melbourne to Heathrow and I was booked into the seat next to Siobhan. I helped her load her hand luggage into the overhead compartment. I admit I noticed she was travelling alone and had no wedding ring.

[Note: his voice was clipped with no obvious humour or emotion—he constantly stared over my shoulder perhaps to avoid looking into my eyes. I looked back at him, deliberately expressionless.]

Cameron: It seems to me a long-haul flight is the true test of whether you'll be able to live with a person. She didn't snore. She could make interesting conversation but didn't speak incessantly. During the flight, she read a book—something about Copenhagen—and a broadsheet newspaper. She was a little shorter than me and looked in good shape. I always notice shoes.

Hers were made of leather. They were good quality and well-polished.

[Note: it seemed the kind of way a marine biologist might describe a specimen he'd caught.]

When the time came to take a taxi from the airport, we delayed our parting. I offered her my phone number and we agreed eating pasta together at a place on George Street sometime soon would be nice. That was how it began. Nothing earth-shattering but it felt to me like a good fit.

[Note: He rested for a long time at this point, and I worried, he might think he'd told me everything I should need to know and he would dry up. I decided prompting was the way to go.]

A.J.: I know a fair bit about Siobhan's background, she was my father's cousin, but I know practically nothing about you.
Cameron: Me? Nothing too special. I'm an only child. My parents died five years before I met Siobhan—a boating accident in Australia when they were on holiday. At the time, I was a reserve soldier, a lieutenant, in the Kings Own Scottish Borders.

A.J.: Still?

Cameron: No, I retired a long while ago, about twenty years. I'd given a decent amount of service by then and had a young family, two girls, with my present wife, Elaine. I didn't want to be away from them for weekends and sucking up vacation time doing service with the regiment.

[Note: I watched him vigilantly. His affect didn't perceptibly change as he tripped from one subject to the other. No love light shone in his eye, even though we were talking about his wife and children. If told I was talking to a sociopath, I would have believed it.]

A.J.: Tell me, did Siobhan ever talk about her brother Aidan?

[Note: In theory, I was leading him into sensitive territory, but without prompting, I doubt whether he'd have mentioned his young, dead brother-in-law. Still no sign of emotion – he swung back in his seat and sipped at his coffee.]

Cameron: She told me what had happened. It was before we met. I know, like everyone else, it was a Para bullet that killed him—shot in the back. And I had to do some thinking for sure when she told me that. It was a big thing, and

I knew it would lie between us. So, tell me, what you already know?

[Note: Smart move to get me to talk and he put his elbows on the table. I thought how effortlessly he could change the subject.]

A.J. What you said about how he died, plus I was named after him, and the Saville enquiry said it was the Paras fault. That's about it.

[Note: I checked his eyes—nothing.]

A.J.: But in the end, you decided to go ahead and get married, so I assume you worked things out between you.

[Note: Cameron shrugged, the mildest version of a shrug you could imagine.]

Cameron: I'd never been stationed in Londonderry. I specialised in coastal defence. She seemed able to put my army career in a different compartment from her home life in Londonderry and Aidan's death. But that's not to say we were going to be stupid about the potential trouble there'd be if anyone there found out she was married to a British soldier.

[Note: If I was a casual onlooker, I wouldn't have been able to tell if he was discussing something life changing, or the price of chicken. He seemed a master at keeping himself in check—or maybe he didn't feel emotion. I started to wonder what life must have been like in his household. Did they ever laugh or let rip with a choice few swear words? What would it have been like with Siobhan who was used to laughter, music and chaos?]

Cameron: After we got married, I got the sense visiting Ireland became no more than an obligation to her. She visited her mother every three months or so. Almost always without me. She came back once and said, they'd sometimes ask her if we planned to start a family and she said the look in her mother's eyes seemed to say, "Are you ashamed of us Siobhan?" She told them we were busy, and it wasn't the time for her to leave her work.

I never met her brother Brendan. Not even at her funeral. People said he was holed up drunk in a bar somewhere.

A.J.: I hope you don't think this is out of order, but what happened on the day she died?

[Note: Again, he focused on the wall over my shoulder.
He waited for a few moments and then plunged in without looking directly at me]

Cameron: It was summer, after we'd been
married for less than a year, I got a
posting to Comox on Vancouver Island.
I liaised with the military there, and
often took part in coastal manoeuvres
with them—usually to do with protecting
the marine environment.
My time was fully occupied on the trip.
Siobhan treated it like a bit of a holiday. She walked or jogged on the
beach, and sometimes worked on a report
for her job. That morning she told me
she wanted to run along the stretch of
coast known as the Royston Wrecks. It
was a quiet place.
Before I left, I went into the bedroom.
She was awake. The police think it was
still early when she reached the public
car park.
The shot must have come from the thick
stand of trees that sat back from the
water.

[Note: as he finished the sentence, he swung back on the
chair and looked up at the ceiling again. I decided to prod
a bit more. I didn't want him to let him go off the boil.]

A.J.: is that all you found out?

Cameron: There is one more thing no one else in the family knows. She'd told me a couple of days before, and it was confirmed by the postmortem. She was about three months pregnant when she was killed. I didn't send the family a copy and they didn't ask for one.

A.J.: I'm sure no one knows about the baby, or they would have told me by now.

[Note: I stopped mostly because I was trying to run quickly through everything I'd heard from my parents and Henry and whether there was a sign someone was keeping quiet about this. I nodded at him. This was the ultimate sign of empathy I could summon up before I blundered on.]

A.J.: That is so sad, and it makes my next question a bit more important in my eyes. Is it true no one has ever been arrested for her murder?"

Cameron: No. Not even a suspect I know of.

[Note: He pulled back in his chair and then righted it again with a bit more force. He pulled himself forward using the table and grabbed his bags. His whole

demeanour said he was bringing things to a close. I sus-pect, forever.]

Cameron: Well, nice to have met you. I hope you got what you wanted.

[Note: he turned without waiting for a reply or offering his hand, left me sitting nursing the dregs of my coffee. I turned off the recorder. He had lost his wife and their un-born baby. I could only assume any emotion I'd seen any evidence of would have been because of that. Even that was hard to detect. I could think of nothing to say that would illicit more.]

END OF TRANSCRIPT

[End Note: I watched him walk away, leading with his shoul-ders, cutting into the crowd. In the forty minutes until my train to Edinburgh was due, I listened again to the recording. I wanted to remember the details. Matching what he was say-ing with the body language I recalled. It seemed every bit as important as what he said. I made my notes ready for the transcript.
I had a clear image of how he habitually swung back on the chair and looked up at the ceiling when he told me anything emotional—especially when he talked about Siobhan's death.]

The train back to Edinburgh headed east through Glasgow and would have passed close to the dance hall where Robert, my mother's dad would have shown off his dancing skills when he'd arrived back from service. I've been told by a local worthy once, the outside might have resembled a bomb site at the time, but the floors shone like glass. Robert, I thought, would have no knowledge of his daughter's story and the drama that now occupied his grandson. I somehow doubted he cared.

My mind turned to mush with the rocking of the train, and I was grateful for the cold air that hit me on the walk back to my flat. Awake now, I called Dad on my cellphone as I climbed up from the platform level.

I opened with, "Guess who I've been with this afternoon."

He didn't seem in the mood to play games and so I went on, "I got to meet Cameron."

"How did it go?" He asked. I could tell by his voice I'd summoned up some curiosity.

"Not sure. He's such a cold fish. Even face to face, I couldn't get a read on any emotion he might have been feeling."

The card I kept to my chest was the news of Siobhan's pregnancy at the time of her death—something to keep until my enquiries were over.

"Sounds like him. So, are you nearly finished your investigations?"

"Is that what we're calling it now, 'investigations?'" I laughed to keep things light.

I added while it was in my mind, "You haven't sent me the contact info for Brendan."

He took that answer as my response to things being over. "I suppose that answers my question."

He let the silence sit for a while. "Wee Patrick says he doesn't move out of Derry much."

"Fine. An email address would be good."

"I'll send it to you this evening. Now, you take care and make sure I know when you're going over there and when you'll be back. I don't suppose you'll have time to go to Newry?"

"I doubt it, but maybe the three of us can go over some time and lay some flowers on the grave, and visit the farm. I think I'll be ready when I get to the end of this."

"Right. I'll mention it to your mum."

It was a dry night. I used the side entrance to exit the station and climbed a steep set of stone stairs up to the level of the St. James Centre. You had to be an Edinburgh native to know that little short cut. You also had to be fond of climbing stairs. I felt righteous as I panted and walked home slowly, thinking about the dream and Cameron. The fact he swung back on the chair stayed with me. I pictured it again, so seemingly casual, used to increase the distance between us and to keep control of feelings. Was he merely a cold fish, or did I have to watch my back because he now knew I was digging into ground he wanted left undisturbed and securely in the past?

I walked towards home and pulled my collar up. I glanced over my shoulder, and as I did, a feeling came over me in that moment that could explain why Dad had left well alone all that time ago. Was he, like me now, scared and full of anxiety for his family?

11. Brendan

Source: Transcript of meeting with Brendan 2011
Time Reference: 1972 – 2011

I booked my flight to Derry for what I optimistically believed would be the last interview I would need to complete my project. The feeling of fear I had after talking to Cameron was still at the back of my mind but did not displace the desire to push on until the end.

On the flight, I made some room in my head for personal matters. By coming here, I'd let down friends and George, my 'someone special.' I was going to have to beg for forgiveness. One day soon, I would be introducing him to my parents. The timing of the impending surprise of my sexuality could have been better, but maybe not. Maybe they might have a better appreciation of honesty when this was over.

I remembered O'Riordan's from the time I went to the bar with Dad to meet Brendan about five years before. Back then, he'd decided it was time to check if his cousin was alive or dead, or what territory between those two states he was inhabiting. No differently to then, I didn't exactly know where he was staying and frankly didn't mind if I ever found out.

I walked past the unofficial sentry in the doorway, a man with two fingers missing on his right hand, a pint and a lit cigarette in his left. I stood inside the main door with one hand in the pocket of my jeans and looked around. The floor was sticky, and the tables matched. The windows were high up with bullseye glass to keep separate the patrons and the outside world of girlfriends, debt collectors and law enforcement.

On my first sweep of the crowd, I didn't spot Brendan, but I'd lingered long enough to stop a few conversations and for the server to walk to my end of the bar and say, "What can I do for you?"

"I'm looking for my uncle, name of Brendan."

This slight distortion of our true relationship saved me from stuttering out something about second cousin once removed. I was betting the way to go was to opt for a relationship easier to work out in the heads of anyone listening.

I can't imagine Brendan was an uncommon name, but I saw a flicker of recognition cross the bartender's eyes. Before I could test this, a raspy voice advancing just ahead of the smell of whiskey and the contents of an ashtray whispered in my ear.

"Hello Aidan m'boy."

I turned and vaguely recognised him—skinny, close cropped grey hair, single earing with a silver crucifix the size of a piece of cutlery hanging from it, leather jacket circa 1980; stiff black jeans, a stranger to laundry soap, ripped but not designer fatigued. He smelled of a lack of self-care. I guessed at his age, sixty something. My dad often referred to him as 'Sid', a nod to Sid Vicious, the punk rock front man. Even in the semi-darkness I could see his skin was sallow and lined with spidery red veins, the whites of his eyes were yellow. Not a well man I guessed. For once I felt well-groomed in comparison.

Brendan pointed me to the bar but hung back making me the one who would be paying by virtue of being the one doing the ordering—for him, a double Irish with a Guinness chaser and a pint of lager for me. Something about the order itself, not only my accent, would have screamed 'relation from over the water' to the other patrons. They muttered but soon enough got back to whatever conversation they had been indulging before, and to a bond with the contents of their own glasses.

The mirror over the gantry was tilted downwards and I managed to catch my own reflection. I had definitely lost weight in recent weeks and my hair looked unkempt. I needed to get back to taking care of myself.

He said to the barman in a loud voice, "Thanks Dieter," and drinks in hand, we headed straight to a corner table with no immediate neighbours.

"German?" I asked, nodding in the direction of the barman.

"Probably. We're proper cosmopolitan here in Ireland now boy; in the EU—freedom of movement and everything else entailed."

At some point, I must have telegraphed how uneasy I was here in this strange bar because Brendan looked over his shoulder to the other patrons and said through a wet cough, "Don't worry about these jokers, they're harmless."

Now it was down to me. I'd practised a few lead-ins to the questions I wanted to ask, and it was time to pick one.

"You'll have heard about the Saville Report?"

"Fuckers." Enough said to update me on his current mood and connection to the issue.

"I'm writing a bit about it."

"Fuck's sake, what hasn't already been said, A.J?" He shifted around in his seat, enough to convince me there was little more to be said on the subject.

If he hadn't been wrecked by drink back in the day, my impression was that he was now. I wasn't sure my dad would recognize him. I inched forward, the better to check his reaction to everything I said. I wanted to pay attention, to give myself the best chance to get to the core of the story he could tell without scaring him out of the door. One mistake on my part, and I was afraid he would be out of reach for good. I got ready to tread carefully.

At the same time, I had an instinct he was the man with a singular connection to Siobhan and the answer to the big questions, how and why and *who*?

I hoped against all hopes I wasn't mistaken because he was the final witness I had on my list. I didn't see him as a relative whose health and wellbeing I should have been concerned about. He embodied my last hope. And I knew I would go on buying him drink, asking him to touch his past, poking at his answers, and indulging my curiosity regardless of what it might take out of him. Maybe later, when I would have to explain to my parents about how the meeting went, I'd sanitize the information about his condition and my investigative technique. I'd pretend it was an interesting chat, and he was glad to unburden himself to a young family member. I'd lie.

My recorder was set on the table and the red light was steady. If he suspected this was a family chat, that piece of equipment probably disabused him of the idea.

Even from our brief chat on the phone to arrange the meeting, he knew what I was there for.

"Before we even start," he said nodding at the recorder, "you can't go publishing names."

I came back at him with, "Surely with Siobhan, Aidan, and your mother dead…"

He didn't let me finish the sentence.

"I'm not worried about my safety. The doctors have given me two or three months—liver's shot. But no matter what with the new peace that was brokered a few years back, there's quite a few hereabouts, prominent men, who wouldn't want themselves attached to previous misdoings. They want to get on, get themselves seats in Stormont and Westminster. I know how determined they are, and I don't want you or yours to go stumbling around and getting yourselves killed."

I felt myself exhale. Proof if proof were needed, that at the heart of this story was a connection to the Troubles.

I tamped down a flash of excitement. "Fair enough," I said.

"Well, I'll answer yer questions, but I'll not give you any names I don't think you should have. So, what exactly is it you're after?"

"Before I start, I want to let you know Mum and Dad have no interest in raking up the past. They're happy with the results of the latest enquiry and how it vindicates what the family have known all along—Aidan was an innocent boy shot down because he happened to be at the demonstration. They've never been as curious as I am about Siobhan's death and what was going on in her life at the time, and if there was a connection to Aidan. I find that strange, and if anything, that's the mystery I'd like to get to the bottom of. It's all about me and my need to figure out what happened and why they don't seem all that bothered."

I paused. He was staring down at the table, swirling the whiskey around his glass. He said nothing in reply, so I went on.

"First, could you go back to the time when Mum and Siobhan visited when they were finishing university? I'd like your take on their friendship and how you found my mum, young Rose?"

"Yer mother, Rose, was not like the people I knew and if I'm being honest, I'd say I was pleased our Siobhan had made a friend that seemed well set up—lived on a farm and rode horses. Perhaps I was a bit worried Siobhan would begin to look down on us, but I soon enough learned I needn't have been concerned."

He then leaned in close to the recorder and spoke more quietly, and I thought it best to let him run with it.

TRANSCRIPT – MEETING WITH BRENDAN.

Right after that summer, time flew. I had no job, and it would be a little

234

while before I started to roadie for the band, you know, The Guttersnipes. Siobhan was in Glasgow studying or some such, and yer mam and Connor were getting close.

And then of course it happened… 1972.

[Note: Long pause—he wiped his nose on his sleeve and as the silence went on, my eyebrows knotted together in tension. I let him have a moment.]

Brendan: On the day our Aidan was murdered, Siobhan'd been staying with us, and that morning she'd set off for the airport to get back to Glasgow. When I waved her off in the taxi, the crowds were beginning to gather outside the flats for the demonstration. It was a big crowd. Young and old. Not the Provos, more the civil-liberties types and the kids who joined in any parade going.

But, Siobhan, didn't make it onto the plane before the news came of the killings, and she came straight back to the house.

[Note: Long pause—he stared at the opposite wall. I was not sure how this was going to go and it was an effort for me to stay silent at this point. I bit my bottom lip and made a spire of my fingers, arms resting on the table. I

consciously relaxed my shoulders, shook out my arms. I hoped he didn't notice.]

Brendan: Can you imagine what the next days were like? It must have been about a month before the funerals. Somehow it was decided there'd be a big service for the majority. Eleven, I think it was. It all passed over my head. People shook my hand as they came and went into the house to pay their respects to my mother. The women from the church brought in food for us and the men brought drink. It was an extended wake. Eventually the coffins were all taken to St. Mary's. That cut down the amount of foot traffic in the house. I was glad of the peace and quiet after things settled.
I'd be a liar if I said I remember Aidan's funeral in every detail, I'd been on a bender for a couple'a days. I believe it was miserable and rainy, it was February after all. It wasn't to be Aidan's funeral alone. It was for all eleven people. St. Mary's is here in the Creggan and from the church they were taken off in processions to be buried.
At some point in the previous days, when I was stumbling around, I looked

into the room where the coffins were laid. There were no flowers, it was feckin' stark. The whole set up made me panic, wanting to run. How could this be for Aidan? It was hardly real to me.

[Note: he stopped for a minute, cocked his head in the middle of the busy bar. I started to wonder what he could hear.]

Brendan: Can you hear the noise out there right now? 'Course you can. When I walked around out there on the day, it was nothing like that. Thousands were gathering, but it seemed deathly quiet--feckin' unnervin'. You couldn't hear traffic or shouting. Nothing.
Now, this wasn't to be the IRA's version of a military funeral. There was no men in masks ready to shoot a volley over Aidan's coffin before the rifle party were spirited away by the crowds. He wasn't one of their boyos and We were never approached by them, thank God. We didn't need them, but I knew they were hanging around in their civvies, paying respects, showing that they saw Aidan's death as part of their fight. And the army stayed away but I'm sure their plain clothes men were there too. Hidden in plain sight.

[Note: he paused here again and looked up at the ceiling for what seemed like minutes but was probably seconds. Maybe he was running his own movie made of patchy memories. I could feel the pain radiating out of him— probably the pain all older brothers who believed they had failed their kid brother would have felt. Then he sniffed before going on.]

God, I must have nearly drunk Derry dry that day. I have huge blanks, but somehow, I got home before we were due to leave for the service and I'm told Mary and Siobhan dressed me in a shirt and tie and then, what did I do? I did a runner, probably so I didn't have to walk Aidan to his grave.

But later in the day, I can't remember when exactly, I got back home, and got sober, quick.

There were people in the house and Siobhan drew me aside. With no preliminaries whatever, our girl asked me to introduce her to the local leader of the Provos. Straight out. And I can tell you, I didn't take another drop that night.

Now, you don't need me to paint you a picture of what was going on then—right after Bloody Sunday. People had to watch themselves. You could die from

238

being in the wrong place at the wrong time. Y'were dodging barricades, some put up by the Brits, some by young lads. I couldn't tell you how many times I had to duck into doorways to avoid bullets, and that was just going down to the boozer or to get the makings of our next meal. And on that very day, the boyos burned the British Embassy in Dublin right to the ground.

The tension was like a weight we carried everywhere. We were stoop-shouldered with it.

It was a living a war zone, and there she was, wanting to get into the middle of it all, or so it seemed to me.

A.J.: Did you know the guy she meant?

[Note: he looked irritated and shook his head either from frustration because I was underestimating his local knowledge or perhaps because I was overestimating it and branding him a terrorist.]

Brendan: Of course, I knew the man she was talking about, but only to nod at like. We weren't on speaking terms. It was common knowledge the boyos had an office over Haggerty's insurance shop. Everyone in the Bogside knew it.

Shit, I didn't mean to say the name there. You be sure to miss the name out Aidan m'boy.

It was the place to go when people were giving you trouble needing, how shall I put it, a local solution. It was the place to report your son missing. People went there to get compensation if a brick thrown by one of their lads broke a window. You should know A.J, where we came from, these were the men who, in reality, policed the place. Not exactly people to mess with.

Her question sobered me up sharpish. At first, I thought I must have misheard her. After all, here was my sister, the university graduate studying for some high-class degree, not a Mary-Hick from these parts.

I said to her, "If I were mad I would." And added, "Not on your life. You get back to Glasgow."

Her reply: "If you won't take me, I'll go there myself and wait 'til I see someone I can have a word with."

"A word about what, Siobhan?"

And the next thing, she grabbed her jacket and walked out of the flat with me hot on her heels.

We walked and walked, with me out of breath, loosening my black tie and asking her to tell me what she was thinking. As we reached the place, Haggarty's, I believe I was literally begging with her not to take another step. I asked her to come into the bar next-door for a drink.

I remember saying, "It'll calm you a bit and we can talk about this some more." I remember her face as if it were yesterday—hair pulled back tight, pinched at the mouth, eyes squinted up like slits.

But she kept her back rigid, face forward and walked up the flight of stone steps to the second floor of the building. The door had no name on it, just a bell to ring. She pushed the button. Someone peered through the spyhole, and I thought it was best if I spoke.

"It's Brendan, Aidan's older brother. I'm here with my sister Siobhan. She wants to talk to himself."

The door opened slightly, and yer man said, "Who is it you want to see?" I knew him from the streets and wasn't impressed with his official-sounding tone.

"Whoever's there," Siobhan piped up. "I've an offer to make."

The man opened the door wide and said something like, "My condolences, Miss.

Please pass on our heartfelt sorrow to your mother. Aidan was a fine boy. God rest his soul. I didn't know him well, but he played a bit of football with my son Donal. Come in and sit down on one of these chairs and tell me what you have a mind to talk to us about."

"Thank you," says she, "but I'm here to see what passes for the boss hereabouts—Captain, Colonel, Major or something?"

"Siobhan, you would need to tell me your business before I could refer you to a senior officer."

Siobhan was always the bold one and she looked the man right in the eye and said, "Right then, tell your boss I want to be of use. I regularly and legitimately go back and forward to Glasgow. I visit my mother here and I study and work there. I've lived more or less full-time in Scotland for four years and have close friends there. I'm under no suspicion. I can move about freely. I'll be going back to Scotland as soon as I help my Ma to settle a bit."

I was thinking at the speed of a madman at this point when a voice came from the doorway leading to an inner office. It was himself. The brother-in-law of the business owner, Haggarty.

"Have you talked about this to anyone else?" He asked

"No, I haven't." she piped up. "Not even my mother. Brendan's the only one who knows I'm here."

"Well lets' talk," he said, inviting us into his office.

[Note: I hadn't experienced that level of tension building up in my body before. Not frustration, it was actual visceral fear. This was a story with bona fide dangerous people involved. I made myself keep looking at Brendan. I didn't want him to ease off and I thought a couple of words from me would help.]

A.J.: Were you shit scared? Did the man look like a gangster?

Brendan: I was trying to keep calm, quite a bit out of my depth and yer man was wearing jeans and a leather jacket—standard Provo gear for the time.

As we were sitting down on a sofa he said, "Firstly, you're a fool if you think no none knows you're here. The Brits have this place under constant watch. So, you'll have been noted, probably photographed. And secondly, do you realise we're all volunteers? All the money we bring in must be dedicated to the armed struggle."

I can't recall her exact words, but the question made her mad and she finished up by saying, "This is about Aidan and Ireland, nothing else."

There was that bitterness in her voice, the kind we Irish get with our mother's milk, and the only thing I remember about the walk home is me telling her it wasn't too late to call it off.

I thought she'd be thinking more clearly the next day.

I was wrong.

[Note: He checked my face for a reaction. I didn't say a thing—now not wanting to interrupt his flow. The silence went on for a while. It was tougher than I'd ever known before to stay silent. Brendan drew something I didn't recognise with the beer sweat on the table.]

Brendan: When she turned up for tea the day after that meeting, she told me she'd gone to the fruit counter in the local supermarket as she'd been told to. Then, a man took her to a house in the suburbs and the commander she met there told her they wanted her to be a courier—to move packages around. The only other thing I remember her saying was she was told to keep away from any kind of trouble and not to draw atten- tion to herself. Then he handed her an

envelope with a cheque made out to my
mother. The story they'd put about to
cover our call at the office, was we'd
gone to ask for a donation to help our
mother with the funeral expenses. De-
positing the cheque would support our
cover story. The Brits were used to the
quasi-charitable arm of the terrorist
organizations.

A.J.: What was going through your head?

Brendan: I convinced myself being a
courier was an innocent enough thing to
do—no harm, no foul. Later on, I asked
her about her instructions. She'd been
told to phone the office from a call
box the day before she planned to return to Glasgow. And they would get a
package to her.

Now, I knew this was her test. On the
day, I waited around the corner of the
office while she went inside, apparently to swear an oath of an alle-
giance. Simple as that, she was in-
ducted into the Derry Brigade of the
Provisional IRA, 'green booked' they
called it.

A.J.: Did you ever get to know what
went on after that?

Brendan: I'm not going to tell you I
wasn't curious, about what happened in
Glasgow, I had a million questions to

ask her when she next came back home. And maybe because I was the only one she could talk to, she didn't seem to mind telling me. So, I got chapter and verse about her first mission, as she called it.

She flew to Glasgow with the envelope hidden among the sweaters in her hand luggage. It would have been her first time back in Glasgow after Aidan's killing.

The next morning, she got a call at her flat from a public phone box. The code words were used, "Can we meet for lunch at the cafe?" And she said something like, "I can be there at noon." Keeping it simple was how she explained the exchange to me. None of that, 'the eagle has landed' crap.

As she told it, exactly at noon, she put the envelope she'd been given in Belfast on the table in the coffee shop. She was around the corner from the university department where she worked. It must have all looked kosher. Her female contact came through the door, brought a coffee, saw the envelope, and sat down with the drink in her hand. She was dressed in the flight attendant uniform of some European passenger airline. The stranger called herself Kelly. I have no idea whether this was her real name, but I think probably not.

The woman apparently had a pronounced Liverpool accent, and she inspected the seal on the package

"I haven't touched it," Siobhan was offended like.

"I can see that," says the Kelly one. And then she tells Siobhan to go to the John Lewis Department Store and purchase a black Samsonite Overnighter with certain locks and trim. Easier to do the swaps if all the couriers used the same bag, she'd said. Kelly's parting words were to let the office know when she was planning a trip to Derry, and to always phone from a public call box, and use a different one each time. This would be because they knew their lines were tapped. She was to say when she phoned, 'my mother wants to come by' and name the date. This told them the day she would be leaving Glasgow. Kelly also said something about being paid if she was ever asked to do a special jaunt but at first, they'd use her normal back and forth trips. She was warned not to visit Derry more than has been her habit in the past year.

I was reassured by what she said—a bit. She wasn't going to be asked to do anything mad, just taking papers and the like back and forth.

A.J.: So you're absolutely sure she was working for the Provos pretty regularly, and you said nothing about it to her or anyone else?

Brendan: I'm as certain as I can be without her telling me every time she did a job for them. And as for me having a say in anything she did, you obviously didn't know her. She had a bull head and made her own plans. Hell, I didn't even want her to go over to St. Andrews. I thought she was too young to be so far away from home. And look where that got me.

Now let me get back to the story while I've still got it in me.

I remember at some point, during the first meeting she told me she asked Kelly what was in the envelope and was told it was two thousand pounds in cash.

Siobhan had said, "You trusted me with that kind of money?"

Kelly looked her straight in the eye and said, "Of course we did. After all, we know where you live."

That was probably the first time when someone else was in control. But she took it from them. Dangerous not to know she was already involved.

[Note: I paused to take this in. The people Brendan was talking about were real. I'd never heard anyone speak about this before—perhaps because Brendan is the only one who knew about it.

Note: His expression had changed over the course of his retelling. His mouth became drawn down, more conspiratorial.]

Brendan: I assumed every time she came over to Ireland, she carried a package in the Overnighter and a handover of some sort took place in cafes, bathrooms or department stores. As far as I know, she never marched in military formation or personally killed anyone. Honestly, I stopped enquiring and the only other time she ever took me into her confidence was over some trip to Newfoundland in Canada. That was paid for by the boyos. She told me that much.

Now, I can guess what you're thinking because I've wondered the same thing myself, was courier work enough to mollify someone with the amount of hate she had. The answer is I don't know for sure. Maybe she'd convinced herself she was getting her payback by backing the people who were doing the shooting. And I know in the back of my mind she was smart enough to realise she would be steering clear of the worst of it if things went south. But on the other hand, I'm not sure. I know the anger I felt and there are a few people hereabouts got a beating they didn't deserve because of how I took it out on them. If you could've seen Siobhan's face the day of the funeral. I think you'd have your doubts too. She looked like someone who could've pulled the trigger. Maybe she made the decision to use her brains and outsmart them. Maybe that gave her the satisfaction she needed. She never spoke enough for me to figure it out.

[Note: Long pause for a coughing fit. I searched in my pocket for a tissue. The only one I could offer was my usual crumpled variety from the bottom of my jean's pocket. He waved it off—I didn't blame him.]

Brendan: And she pulled back from people from her past, became distant with people who weren't suffering like her family were. After a few drinks one

Christmas, she ranted on a bit about how Rose never knew how lucky she was— maybe born illegitimate, but totally landing on her feet. And how it was as if God looked down on her and decided she would from henceforth be blessed. She sounded none too friendly as she went on about how the polio made her thin and all this meant was that she was the kind of female men wanted to protect. Even Connor.

The only other job she told me about, was that trip to Canada, with your mother—the one she'd been speaking badly about. It was one of those special jobs and right here I'd have to say, if she cared about protecting her friend Rose, she didn't show it.

A.J.: I'd like to hear what you know. I've only had my mother's version.

Brendan: I can't remember exactly when or all the details, but I don't think it was long after she first started, maybe the Spring of the next year. The deal, she told me, was to pick up cash-donations coming to the Provos from North America. She said going with Rose to give her a cover—two university friends travelling from Glasgow to New-foundland on a vacation.

She told me she took the overnighter full of books over to Canada, tossed them on the other side and filled it up with cash for the return. I said to her I found it a bit hard to believe they were relying on actual cash being lugged across the Atlantic and she said there were other means used by the cause, but this was spreading the risk. I don't remember if she did any more of those trips, but I know she was travelling a bit at some point, and this was meant to do with her university work. More, I don't know.

A.J.: So, how did you think things changed after she met Cameron?

Brendan: Well, to be honest, after she met Cameron, we grew further apart, and I didn't spend much time wondering if she was still working for the boyos. Things seemed to be going well for her. I was with the band by this point, and so I left it at that. I always think bad news finds you soon enough. I didn't think twice about her new husband. I thought he was a Scot, but some of those are as committed to the Republican cause as we Irish are. Ever heard the saying, 'ask no questions…'

A.J.: …you'll get told no lies.'

Brendan: That's the one.

A.J.: By the way, Cameron's English.

Brendan: Hmph! Is that right?

Let's get on with this.

Every now and again, someone 'round here would ask how married life what suiting her, and I'd always say 'fine' because I didn't really have a clue. I didn't want people knowing our business.

I guess you want to know, do I think if the boyos knew anything about what she was about? I can tell you I'm certain she told them nothing about getting married. Maybe because she thought it would keep her and Cameron safe. If she did, she was a bigger fool than I gave her credit for.

I would say, with the rage in her, it was entirely possible for a time she even hated Rose, and so I doubt she would tell her any secrets. In her eyes, Rose was a Brit who paid her taxes and voted for the people who ordered the army to enter our homes and our lives to kill immature, stupid young boys. Maybe it made it easier for her to think of Rose as just another asset, not as a friend.

[Note: He leaned back. My chance to ask some questions, but first I shuffled off to buy another round of drinks—mostly as an offering to keep him going. I had a lot to slot into place: her hatred—however temporary, did that make sense of her absences, her change of heart—then her wanting Mum and Dad to stand up for her at her wedding.
I settled back into my seat and noticed his face had become more drawn and yellowish in the shaft of light coming in.]

Brendan: I can't be much longer, A.J. I need to get home for my drugs and a bit of a kip.
A.J.: Sorry if I've tired you out. And I've only a couple more questions… How much do you think Cameron knew about her past?
Brendan: No idea. And for the record, I know he was a soldier but didn't find out until after the funeral, and I can't for the life of me remember who told me. I've no idea how anyone would have found out, but they had. I heard the Cameron one made off sharpish after the service. No wonder, at first, I thought he was just a rude bastard.
My mother was the only one to talk to him on the phone after that. She was looking for any updates on how the

254

police were doing with finding Siobhan's killer. He had the contacts in Canada and so she relied on him for info. Not that she got much.

Brendan: I thought about it, and if he was a British agent set out to assassinate her, my thinking is, he took too long. And it's not as if he needed to marry her to get a chance to kill her. That's my opinion anyway.

A.J.: I found out from him Siobhan was pregnant, about three months, when she was shot.

[Note: a pause while he did that swinging on the back legs of his chair, and I noticed he stared at the ceiling. Thinking of Cameron, I wondered if this was typical of men of that age. It seemed to take for ever for him to right the chair and look at me.]

Brendan: Don't say that Aidan. Are you sure?

[Note: I nodded, and he looked up at the ceiling again. I blew out some air through my lips, to keep from barking my frustration at him. I wanted a reaction. There was silence for a moment longer.]

Brendan: Well, that settles it for me. I can't see the man killing his own wife especially if she was carrying his baby.

A.J.: I'm coming around to the same view. So, d'you think it was an IRA hit?

[Note: At this point, a fat guy in jeans with his belly pushing over his belt approached us. I was barely able to contain my annoyance, but I smiled—looking acidic, I'm sure.]

Haggarty: The name's Haggarty. I'm an old friend of Brendan's. And you are?" His right hand with at least three gold rings on the fingers extended toward me.

[Note: The name immediately rang a bell—the insurance man? Not at all the kind of lean hard looking man from the 1970s who's picture I had in my mind. He was wearing a good quality thick cotton shirt, a grey pullover and well-polished leather brogues. I had to remind myself of his possible backstory –unbidden, my shoulders became tense again.]

A.J.: A cousin.

[Note: I shook his pudgy hand as he continued to stare directly into my eyes but said nothing else. He left us after pressing his fat fingers into Brendan's shoulder.]

Brendan Interview conclusion – from memory

Brendan: To my way of thinking, you've got your stone-cold hit man possibility on one hand, then you've got the kind of red-hot avenger type of killer who has a long memory and who will hunt his kill no matter how long it takes.

A.J.: And why d'you think they did it in Canada?

Brendan: Well, for sure they have their people over there and it created distance from any suspects in Ireland.

A.J.: The one big thing that's still stuck in my mind is, did you ever think they would come for you? After all, you knew she was involved with them and how she'd joined them.

[Note: Brendan tossed his head back and laughed, causing himself a coughing fit. Then he leaned forward to look at me.]

Brendan: It crossed my mind—course it did, but I was on the move with the band at the point she went AWOL. They would have known I hadn't seen her for a couple of years at that point and probably knew she kept her cards close to her chest. And I think they had bigger fish to fry. Spending any energy on me probably would have been low on their priorities. And I was quite glad for it to stay like that. I never gave into the temptation to ask them what they knew—self-preservation. I was happy for them to think of me as the black sheep of the family.

And, of course when Mary, my mother, passed away, right after your own grandmother, I had even less reason to hang about here in Derry.

You know, I always wanted her, Mary, to go and stay with her folks in Newry, but she said she wouldn't be able to stick it, living on a farm. She liked the city and she told me once, "South Armagh is every bit as dangerous as Derry—when I die, I want some friends and company around me." I couldn't argue with her, but even so, I worried about her being alone.

Right, are we done?

[Note: At that moment I wondered if Dad had the same instinct as Brendan had. It was one explanation for his evasiveness: his protection of Mum from men who would want people to be silenced if they knew too much.

Maybe they both were scared of what they'd find out if they started to dig around and uncovered what she was up to. Again, lives could be put at risk—their own, their family's. They weren't trying to maintain a rosy glow around Siobhan. It was more pragmatic self-preservation.

And yet, the people who really benefited from their years of silence were those who wanted to put their own activities through a spin cycle. It would not suit for there to be a close look to see if she was shot in 1977 at the height of the trouble as a form of military discipline.

The truth could be inconvenient for current repentant politicians who were at that time, up to their necks in organising and carrying out violence to maintain discipline in the ranks.

I couldn't wait to get back to the hotel room to get these thoughts down while they were fresh, but I had one last question.]

END OF TRANSCRIPT

Brendan got up and interrupted my thoughts. His chair scraped across the floor as he rose unsteadily.

259

"Just tell me." I got up to keep his eyes level with mine. "Are my family in danger? Do the boyos know about us—do they think she might have given us information?"

He opened his mouth and seemed to wave me away before his knees buckled. I ran around the table but not in time to stop his head hitting the floor. I dialled for an ambulance knowing full well it was too late.

I phoned Dad right away and we agreed I should stay in Derry, go to the hospital with Brendan's body and start to deal with the formalities.

The cause of death, in short, was heart failure secondary to liver cancer.

Over the next few days, plans were made for a cremation and for Dad to come over. We would be joined by Wee Patrick and Fergal. Some agreement happened without my knowing, and only men came to the funeral. On the other hand, that might have been an Irish thing.

The Funeral Mass was sparsely attended—us four, a woman wearing a black lace head square, and sitting right at the back the pudgy man with plenty of gold on display. At the conclusion, the priest walked ahead of us to the back of the church.

He passed the woman and nodded a greeting. "Constance."

She nodded back as he passed

The man, Haggarty, skipped out ahead of the priest and was talking to a nun who was staffing a table at the back selling religious trinkets.

At the doorway, the priest turned nodded to the team of funeral directors and told us he'd meet us at the crematorium. We were not going for the procession up the aisle, the coffin carried by relatives. We were paying our respects, but letting the professionals do the lifting and toting. The priest might have expected us to lay on a car but if he did, he would have been disappointed. We weren't working off life insurance money here. The family had all pitched in to cover the costs.

Wee Patrick drove us in a grey S.U.V., we looked respectable, with suits and overcoats on. I bought mine specifically for the occasion.

The day was sunny, but the thermometer was heading downwards. None of us were hanging about.

At the back of the crematorium building, Dad went discreetly over to the priest and handed him a white envelope containing cash. Haggarty looked on from the doorway. For all the world, it was like a scene from a Mafia movie where a cut of some deal was being handed over to a lieutenant or a Don. It was the well-rehearsed gesture of making a gift to the priest for the attendance and personal services the church didn't allow him to charge for.

The priest asked if there was to be a meal and when he was told we were going for a pub lunch he bowed out. No doubt believing there was something better on offer elsewhere.

As we made our moves toward the door, Haggarty extended his hand. Fergal shook it and said, "Thanks for coming."

Haggarty replied, "I'm sorry for your loss. I've known the family for years, from when they stayed in the Bogside, but I don't believe I know much of you gentlemen."

"We're his cousins," said Wee Patrick.

"From the country I expect?"

"That's right." If Wee Patrick or any of the other two knew who he was, they did a great job of covering it up.

He came to me last. "We met that day in the bar. It would've been quite a shock for you—him keeling over like that."

"I knew he was sick but still..."

"I hear you're a writer."

"That's me." I knew he would've seen my recorder on the tabletop. "I was getting some information about his days with the band. I'm hoping to do something on the punk era in Ireland and Scotland. Handy having a family member who was right there."

"It sure would be," Haggarty said. His eyes scanned my face, and I was glad when Dad intervened.

"We should be going. I'm sorry we haven't laid on anything, but we've all had to travel and there was no time to do much more than the basics."

"Understood."

He watched us leave and didn't move until our car drove passed where he stood.

No one inside of the vehicle said anything until we were through the gates and on the main road. We exchanged looks. I believe we all knew who he was and why he had turned up to the funeral of a whiskey-soaked ex punk band roadie. Without him saying a thing, we knew he wanted to draw a line under Siobhan and her family's story.

In Ireland not asking, not knowing, and not telling still comes naturally. It's how people kept breathing.

12.   The Phone Call

Source: From memory
Time Reference: present

After the conversation with Brendan and Cameron, I pulled away from Mum and Dad as I processes the information. The transcripts made with my fancy new software and my notes were fresh. I could refer to them to refresh my memory of what they said, and how they said it.

For a while I maintained 'radio silence'. I didn't want Mum to have any more influence on what I was going to write than she had already done by virtue of owning so much of the early details. I didn't want Dad to notionally wag a finger at me, warning me not to upset my mother.

However, even Dad didn't try to contact me. He must have had some instinct to leave me to my process, and I was grateful for that.

Eventually, without phoning them I sent an email with a full copy of my notes attached. Until then, the manuscript sat on my laptop, unpublished, even to the point of postponing sharing it with those closest to the event.

There was no long explanation in my covering email, it was more or less limited to an invitation to contact me after they read it through. I said I had no immediate plans to use the information; I was leaving things to settle before I took any other steps.

Three days later, when I got home from work, the phone was ringing, it was Mum.

"I remembered something," was all she said. No hello. No preamble. I was surprised she was the one to break the silence. I had thought it would be Dad, he was always the one to run interference—almost always somewhere in the background or as a quiet sentry while Mum and me talked.

"Right," I said, slipping out of my shoes, leaving them in the middle of the kitchen floor, "give me a second to close the door. I'm just home."

She began after a short pause. "You know that Newfoundland trip, I remembered something but didn't say when I was first talking to you about it."

"Okay, I'm listening." I said as I walked to the living room and sat on the sofa and put my legs over the arm—a good position to flop backwards when I felt like it.

264

"When we went over, Siobhan had an overnight case with her that she left behind the desk. She told me she was putting it out of the way so she wasn't tempted to do work all of the time. So, I thought it was to do with some paper or other she was working on."

Mum paused and I checked if she was still on the line.

"Yeah, I'm here," she said. "One day toward the end of the trip Siobhan went out, she said she was going to post a letter. I happened to look out of the window and in the car park, I saw her with the case talking to a man all dressed for golf. He swapped what looked like the identical case with her and she came right back in. A few minutes later she was back in the room."

She had my full attention. "Did you say anything to her?"

"Only, 'did you get your letters off?'"

"What did she say?"

"I think she said, 'Yes.' Nothing else."

Really, the question for me was, "Didn't you think it was odd?"

Mum waited a long time before she answered, "I remember wondering a bit, I didn't want to question her. Things were tenuous having so recently got back on an even keel. So, I pushed it away to the back of my mind."

There were a few more moments of silence. I could hear her breathing and I bided my time.

Mum spoke again, "But as soon as I read what you found out from Brendan, it kind of fell into place."

"What are you thinking now?" I asked.

"Now? I don't know it matters, but I think she may have used me and your dad to cover up stuff she was doing for the IRA—I mean transporting stuff like a courier. But what would we even do

265

with a snippet like that when she's dead and the case probably long forgotten? And could we help catch her killer by passing on what little we know?"

I drew in my breath to get ready for a moment I hadn't been ready for when I walked in the door and sat down.

"But if only for your own peace of mind, tell me how you feel about her. She was a friend, Dad's cousin. She took you to Canada on a trip almost certainly to make her look like an innocent traveller when she was probably collecting funds for the IRA."

Mum interrupted, "But that's it. At worst she was a courier. You haven't found anything out about her being involved in violence or gunrunning."

It's common for people to talk about seeing red when they get angry, but for me, all the colour drained out of the room, I swung my legs around so I was facing forward, and I heard myself say, "For Christ's sake what do you think the money was used for? There's an expression I think fits here—it's called 'wilful blindness'. It means you won't look at the possibilities you find difficult, but here's a newsflash. In 1972 the IRA were using sticks of gelignite and nails taped together. The boyos would light the detonator and then run like hell. But by the time Siobhan was killed they had Semtex, automatic rifles, all the armour piercing bullets they could wish for. And where did it all come from? Where do you think they got the money?"

I didn't stop to give her a chance to answer.

"Some of that ordinance and the training came from Libya. And in case you don't make the connection for yourself, that's the same country that supposedly sponsored the terrorists who blew up the plane over Lockerbie. That was where the money was going

266

to. World-wide terrorism. If it wasn't the Libyans, it was sure as hell some other radicals."

I stopped. My breath was shallow and at the other end there was a terrible silence. The anger, let go in a burst, was being replaced by a cool need to reason with her, to have her move to a better understanding of her own position and the role she played in hiding the truth.

I could hear the rhythm provided by the Edinburgh rain on my window before the silence was broken.

Mum spoke as I sipped the coffee I'd brought home with me, quickly going cold. It was clear from her breaking voice she was probably shocked and fighting tears.

"But all of that sounds nothing like the Siobhan I knew. Nothing," she eventually managed to get out.

I was dead calm, I was tempted to drill home my points, believing they would lead to a certain peace, but now, over the telephone, I was asking her to give up something from the depth of her fears, when I couldn't see her reaction. Apparently, this was going to be the time to have the confrontation previously avoided or steered around but which was right at the base of my dissatisfaction with the equivocation I'd detected as a younger man and couldn't make sense of.

I let out a breath slowly. "I'm sorry we're doing this on the phone. But now we've started I want to get it all out."

I didn't allow her to speak even though I heard her inhale, readying herself.

I went on, my voice now low and calm. "You stuck to your opinion of her, based on a girlhood friendship and the few visits between Aidan's death and her own—a time when she was deep in grief and maybe in anger. Do you think you might only be looking at what you want to see?"

I paused for a while to let her think about that. "Here's what I believe. Your refusing to let go of the Siobhan you got to know as a carefree student is making it impossible to recognise and accept the Siobhan driven mad by sorrow and anger. The one, in the final analysis, is the Siobhan who ultimately learned to forgive if only to save herself and her sanity."

Now I could hear the sobs on the other end of the phone before I softly brought what I had to say to a close. "Mum, it's time for you to embrace that Siobhan and accept her for what she was."

I let the sobs roll a bit more and heard my father's footfall in the background before I said, "We will all be the better for acknowledging this part of the story for what it is. Someone murdered Siobhan as a consequence of the choices she made in her life. She was someone I didn't get the opportunity to know, and you have been standing in the way—just by being evasive."

I heard something indistinguishable on the other end of the phone.

I said, "Can I speak to Dad." I knew I might as well get over and done with—the explaining why I'd made my mother cry and dealing with my guilt about how I'd gone on the attack when I knew their prior motivation around Siobhan's story might have been partly out of fear for our safety.

Coda

On the ferry trip, Dad said, "I suspect the people who could do something about her murder know all the stuff you found out. They aren't going to do anything about it or they'd've done it already."

I thought about that and said, "You're right. There's too much Irish politics of a sensitive nature going on for now: what the secret services knew or didn't know, the jiggery-pokery around foreign money, and the now fallen dictators. But I guess the last thing for us is to come to terms with our feelings about Siobhan. After all, that's all that's within our control."

We talked softly of her mind turned, radicalised by sorrow, then rescued, however briefly, by a love we didn't understand. I told them of her pregnancy, and I saw in their faces, genuine grief. This seemed like a change to me.

They asked if I believed Cameron and I had no hesitation in saying I did.

My mother turned her tearful face away and looked out at the window being lashed by rain and sea water. My father steepled his fingers and then laid his hands on the table, staring at them in silence. For once he didn't seem to feel the need to put a protective arm around her, and I didn't feel the need to be on the attack. The world seemed to have tilted slightly.

"I'm sorry to be the one to tell you. I heard it directly from Cameron; and it was a piece of information he didn't need to tell me, but it was why I've become convinced he wasn't responsible for her death. The fact he told me, how he told it, and how I could be convinced he'd not kill his unborn child."

The atmosphere between us was adult, earnest, and I covered Dad's hands with mine, Mum placed one on top. I let that tableau rest for a moment in the middle of the busy ferry crossing. The truth had transformed us.

I got up my courage. "When I come for Christmas, I'd like to bring a special friend. His name's George."

Dad took Mum's hand. He smiled and took charge. "It's about time."

Mum stayed quiet and looked out of the window again.

November was waiting for us in Derry. The cold came up from underground. The mist wrapped around the walls and buildings, the wind whipped the cold into any exposed skin and made the eyes sting with tears. In the taxi we passed the men in the city centre on

lifts, putting up Christmas lights on the lamp standards, soon to bring some cheer to the greyness of winter. The new footbridge, The Peace Bridge, across the Foyle caught my eye. It was being called a handshake between the east and west side of a divided city.

Finally, we asked the driver to take us past a mural we hadn't seen before—a black and white tribute to the fourteen who died on Bloody Sunday. In a city famous for its street art, this had a more professional quality to it.

Derry was changing, but our last call of the day meant a visit to the past.

Stamping our feet to keep the blood flowing, my parents and I stood in the Bogside at the memorial to the dead of Bloody Sunday. The Rossville Flats were long gone, demolished twenty years after they had welcomed their first tenants. No one wanted to live there after that day. The greyish limestone obelisk set in a memorial garden was a simple and respectful reminder of that January carnage.

I lightly supported Mum's elbow as she limped to place four red roses on the steps.

She spoke to me. "It's only right to leave our flowers here. One way or another life ended at this place for Aidan, Mary, Brendan and for Siobhan."

Dad added, "Many, many others too."

THE END

Acknowledgements

I want to thank the members of the New West Writers Group here in B.C. for sticking with me and helping me to keep working at this novel. I changed my mind about it at regular intervals and so their forbearance has been admirable.

My editor and the person who has largely managed the publication has been my good friend Marlet Ashley. Anyone who knows her would think she had enough on her plate dealing with her own writing and artwork. But I have to give her a huge thank you for putting time aside for me. This would not have come to fruition without you.

About the Author

Elizabeth was born in Lanarkshire, Scotland and graduated with an LLB from Edinburgh University. She worked for many years in the social services sector. In the early 90's she moved with her family to British Columbia, calling the move 'a bit of an adventure'. Elizabeth says, "people need to appreciate that I cannot stay poe-faced for long – it is both a blessing and a curse."

The *Evolution of Sarah* was her first novel and she has completed a second project, which explores deception and tells stories of betrayal. Her second takes the three Musketeers and fires them into twenty-first century Edinburgh—and one of them has PTSD.

Radicalisation is her third project.

In the reductive way of Twitter, she describes herself as: Canada dwelling, Scotland originating, Jazz loving, mother, grandmother and raconteur.

Twitter: @sosbetty

Manufactured by Amazon.ca
Bolton, ON

27158207R00166